# Confessions of A Map Dealer

Also by Paul Micou

*The Music Programme*
*The Cover Artist*
*The Death of David Debrizzi*
*Rotten Times*
*The Last Word*
*Adam's Wish*
*The Leper's Bell*

PAUL MICOU

# Confessions of A Map Dealer

HARVILL SECKER
LONDON

Published by Harvill Secker 2008

2 4 6 8 10 9 7 5 3 1



First published in Great Britain in 2008 by
HARVILL SECKER
Random House, 20 Vauxhall Bridge Road
London SW1V 2SA

www.rbooks.co.uk

Addresses for companies within The Random House Group Limited can be found at: www.randomhouse.co.uk/offices.htm

The Random House Group Limited Reg. No. 954009

A CIP catalogue record for this book is available from the British Library

ISBN 9781846551499

The Random House Group Limited supports The Forest Stewardship Council (FSC), the leading international forest certification organisation. All our titles that are printed on Greenpeace approved FSC certified paper carry the FSC logo. Our paper procurement policy can be found at www.rbooks.co.uk/environment

Printed in Great Britain by
Clays Ltd, St Ives plc

For my parents

# London, 12 September

Henry Hart and Darius Saddler, friends since childhood, meet at the bar of the Brasserie Pierre in Belgravia. They last saw each other thirteen months ago. Hart wears a dark blue linen suit over a tired white shirt, without a tie, and he drinks red wine. Saddler wears jeans, black loafers, a crimson polo shirt, and he drinks champagne. Hart is visibly tense, while Saddler appears relaxed, even languid. Hart is trim, dark-haired, of medium height and pale. Saddler is taller, has light blond hair, and sports a long-term tan. Both men are thirty-eight years old.

— I think I'm losing my sense of humour, Saddler.

— How bad is it?

— I'm finished. My accountant doesn't see a way out.

— Bankruptcy?

— That was the easy part, and it happened four months ago.

— And no progress in that time?

— If digging a deeper hole is progress, then I've made progress.

— Is Mary au fait?

— Christ, yes. Even the children know.

— I've only been vaguely aware that things weren't going well. What was the tipping point?

— Let's start at the beginning, Saddler. My first mistake was to be heterosexual. If I hadn't been heterosexual I never would have married – you know how I adore Mary, but you'll grasp my point. And if not married, childless. And if childless, not facing an avalanche, an *avalanche* of debt, present and future, that I will never be able to pay off. If I'd been like you—

— Yes, yes.

— I'd at least be able to slink off into oblivion like a man without hurting three other people who still, believe it or not, love me.

— So your being heterosexual was the first error?

— Yes. The second mistake was to be middle class.

— Mustn't blame yourself for that, nor for being heterosexual. Both conditions happen to a lot of people.

— And I don't blame you for being homosexual and mysteriously classless. You couldn't help it. It's just that these qualities seem to have worked in your favour. You'll never know the sweet agony of keeping up with these people, these *parents*.

— You're calling me irresponsible.

— No, I'm calling you *not* responsible. You're blameless, and you're my best friend.

— Thank you.

— You're welcome. It's only because we've known each other since we were children that I can vent to you this way, and only to you – we're not in competition. The fact is, I'm a disgrace to my class. I've let down my family. One early solution – which Mary first suggested, in fact – was that we could veer left, politically, and pretend that we were sending the girls to state schools on principle.

— Unthinkable.

— Obviously. Mary and I laughed at the idea one second after it was proposed. Then there was the selling-up-and-going-to-France concept – which was more like it, except that I had nothing left to sell up. You're paying for the drinks, by the way.

— I know.

— And any eventual food.

— Sure. And taxi fare.

— Thank you.

— So you've mentioned the two elements that were out of your control – heterosexuality and class. Where else did things go wrong?

— I chose a losing business. And I made a terrible misjudgement.

— It was good at the beginning, as I recall.

— Great fun. Dipping my toe in, saving some cash, making my first independent deal – a Portuguese map of a part of the coast of Taiwan. Beautiful. I thought the business was perfect, that it was automatic. I knew from experience that I was unsuited to any kind of office work. No good in groups. I would be my own man. You've known I wanted to live that way, since we were about fifteen years old. The plan was that I would drive around Europe to conventions and make deals over coffee, my car boot crammed with valuable maps.

— That's what you did, isn't it?

— For five glorious years. I relished the study of history and cartography. A lot of it was trading at first – no money changed hands. "I'll give you my this for three of your that." And the car boot got filled. And I'd go somewhere else and cash in and start over. That's the sport of it. And believe me, it was all very honourable. A bit like Olympic fencing. You know, you shake hands afterwards and remain friends.

— I never fenced.

— Well. The point is you don't take advantage, not really. It's like any salesman. You can rip people off a few times, but you'll ruin your reputation. You'll be found out. It's pure in that way. I'll happily tell you my philosophy on that score. Maybe someone comes to me with an item they've inherited, or found in their attic. They want to know if I think it might be valuable. People are so full of hope. I'll say, "Could be," which is the honest truth, even if my heart is already thudding against my ribs and I know there's a fifty-fifty chance I'm looking at a treasure. I may already have a buyer in mind. If the person asks, "Will you buy it?" I'll say, "Yes."

If they ask outright how much I think it's worth, I'll say that will require study. It might take weeks. This is the honest truth. They rarely want the hassle. You'd be amazed how often they'll say, "Would you give me ten thousand quid for this map?" And the next thing they know they have a cheque in their hands and I have my treasure. If they take me up on the lengthy valuation, again I will tell them the truth. I'll come right out and say, "I think it's worth one hundred thousand pounds, and I'll sell it for you at ten per cent commission." That is the way I have always operated. Straight as anything. That is . . . until recently, but I'll get to that.

— So there's a built-in limit, a self-imposed limit, a self-interested limit to how badly you'll rip someone off?

— In a nutshell. But there are other, less measurable constraints. For example, the Taiwan map. I knew there was a man, vastly wealthy, who wanted that map. I mean he *craved* that map. I told him that the Taiwanese government might also be interested. You know, they'd put it in a museum or a state building. And they, too, had deep pockets, at least culture-wise. He said he wanted it for himself, to have in one of his houses. I knew how rich he was. He could have paid ten times what I wanted without batting an eye. And yet he wouldn't do it. That was a bit of an epiphany. I wondered if that's how people got rich in the first place. He thought he knew the map's value, and he wouldn't pay a penny more even though he easily could, and would have owned the map for all time. He wasn't mean – he gave millions away to charities – but for an object that he would own he could not permit himself to pay over the odds.

— Did you lower the price?

— I sold to the government.

— For an astronomical sum?

— Enough to get a mortgage on a studio flat in Battersea. And a little left over to buy more maps. That was twelve years ago. And I had a fair run for a few years more. In the meantime I got married.

— And needed a bigger place to live.

— Exactly. This seemed doable. And I worked very hard to make it happen.

— And then the children came along.

— Right again. And, at the same time, a horrible invention called the Internet. This took all of the sport and honour I mentioned out of the equation. Now you might be in Antwerp offering an old colleague a signed fifteenth-century Ferrero of the Antilles, and with a few taps on his keyboard he tells you to fuck off because, for one, it's a contemporaneous copy and, two, the cartouche was forged two hundred years later and, three, there are two more of them that have been sold for a quarter of the price you're asking. There was no more shaking of hands after deals. Most people worked from home, they didn't meet each other anymore. They weren't gentlemen Olympic fencers, they were staring at each other through computer screens and calling each other liars. It became a video game.

— But why couldn't you play the video game?

— I thought I could, but then along came the Hawaiian map.

— Oh yes. I know a little about this part.

— I know you do, but when I told you about that it was happening to me at the time, and I was putting a brave face on things. You remember I had a German partner?

— Andreas. I met him a couple of times.

— Andreas. And he and I had gone in fifty-fifty on a map we found in Lisbon – actually he found it. We bought it together for two hundred thousand pounds each. A shocking sum, especially now, for which I spent everything I had, and I went ahead and remortgaged the house. I didn't see this as much of a gamble. The rest of my business was working well enough to tide me over until we sold the Hawaii and made our profit. Andreas took every precaution in transporting the map – which is rather small, about a foot square – to his Milan bank and popping it into the safety-deposit box. I thought it was going to be my next Taiwan, times twenty. I thought I'd find a rich Hawaiian or the US government itself to double our money within a couple of years, if we went softly. We hadn't tricked the people in Lisbon, or not very much. We paid nearly what they were asking, but we knew they hadn't tried the Hawaiian state or the US federal government. So let's say Andreas and I took a little advantage of not-very-sophisticated Portuguese neophytes who had not been in the business very long, but we made them rich. Fair is fair. And here's a thought for you: owning something like an antique map – or a great painting, or a manuscript of some kind – is a bit like holding it hostage, if you're a dealer. That's what I realised early on. You're almost saying, "Pay what I'm asking for this thing you desire, or it will be destroyed." You're not *really* going to destroy it, but you're going to leave it in a bank where it has literally no value, as if it had been destroyed. Unfortunately, sometimes the people you're figuratively blackmailing say, as it were, "Go ahead and shoot the hostage." The world doesn't change just because one rare map that no one knew about ceases to exist. Nobody gave a damn about the Hawaii. For the longest time I thought we could tough it out – and I was right, in a way. A Japanese businessman wanted the map, we heard, for some sort of creepy Pearl Harbor reason. We'd have sold it for less than the buying price, to tell you the truth. We needed to get rid of the Hawaii. So Andreas goes and fetches the map from Milan, takes it to California, where the Japanese man was at the time, shows it to him, has all the provenance documentation . . . I really should have gone on the trip with Andreas. He's too soft. He let the Japanese guy have the map for twenty-four hours. The man wanted to "live" with the map. So he lives with the map and comes back to Andreas to seal the deal. I swear to God, he had the cheque half written out, Andreas had his sweaty hand ready to accept it, and the Jap's phone rings. His people have made enquiries about our Hawaii.

— Fake?

— No, not a fake. We're better than that, Saddler . . . Oh, all right, yes, a fake, in a way. In that it wasn't unique, it wasn't the first, it was thirty years younger. What was most galling was that the Jap's boys figured this out on their computers, without even the original map in their hands. Andreas and I had scoured the world for this information, and the Jap's boys got to the truth in about ten hours. I honestly thought of giving up the business. If we could make such an elementary mistake and lose everything, what was the future? But I had no choice. I had no other skills. It's a small world I work in – or worked in. Everyone in the fraternity knew how badly Andreas and I had fucked up.

— What happened to the Hawaii?'

— I sold my half to Andreas for three thousand quid. He still holds out hope. He's thinking of having it X-rayed. "There might be a Caravaggio underneath," he says. With my luck, there will be. Another round?

— I'll get them.

— . . .

— Here you are, Hart. Shall we move to another table? There's a draught here by the door.

— Fine.

— This is better.

— Saddler, listen. I'm going to tell you something I haven't even told Mary. And it isn't about the business. The business, she knows about. But this problem, or this series of problems, you're the only one I think I *can* tell.

— I don't want to jump the gun, Hart, but what's her name?

— It's not like that. You'll have to bear with me. The very least of it is that I am being blackmailed, stalked and physically threatened, and I have been for nearly a year. That's part of what has bled me dry.

— You have my full attention.

— You'll understand that I'm only telling you this story because I have to tell *someone*. It's been eating away at me. I've thought about the events so hard, for so long, I've lost perspective. I'm hoping you're going to say I'm a fool and I can ignore it. But like any sort of . . . *festering worry*, I've made it worse by keeping it secret. I think so, anyway. You can be the judge.

— I'll do my best.

— Well, here goes, then. You will remember I stayed with you for a couple of nights down in France. At your ridiculous house.

— Worst mistake of my life, that house. I still haven't sold it.

— Oh, I dined out on that place for a while. "I've stayed at Saddler's chateau . . ."

— It isn't a chateau. That's only how it's advertised.

— It looked like one to me. And my stay with you is going to enter into this story.

— Uh-oh.

— As you'll recall, I was down there reconnoitring property for myself, when Mary and I were in the doomed sell-up-and-leave-England phase of the money crisis. After I left you, I drove in a direction and for a distance that I thought would bring property prices down by roughly half. Two days later, having visited a dozen houses, I believed I'd found my bracket. I began to poke about the little town of St-Vuis – do you know it?

— Yes. They make a lot of doilies. And you told me you were going there.

— That's the spot. It was so blasted hot, I was glad I hadn't brought Mary and the girls along – that is, even if I could have afforded to. I found a cheap room in an old hotel not far from the centre of town. Quiet place. My room, on the second floor, looked out on a small park. More of a courtyard, or a quad, really. Call it a garden. I didn't even know how it was reached, and it didn't seem to be attached to the hotel. It contained a not-very-well-mown lawn and one giant tree that hung over the dry grass from a corner – I'm not good at the names of trees, probably a plane tree. When I first arrived at the hotel there was no one in the garden. I went out and spoke to just two estate agents during the afternoon, and visited three appalling houses. I felt affronted that the agents thought I could live in places like that. You know how they are: each house has a feature they want you to focus on. "You're going to love the tree-lined drive," they say, having sized you up as the sort who would love a tree-lined drive. And the drive leads up to a wretched shack still under reconstruction. When I told one of them what I did for a "living", he drove me out to a place where I was simply going to love the library. He meant well, but all the house *was* was a library. The gloomiest place you've ever seen, with an old man standing in it pleading with his eyes for me to like it. I left there depressed and went back to my hotel with a sandwich and a bottle of wine. I remember opening the window – remember how hot it was – and looking out into the quad. Still no one there. I ate my sandwich and drank the whole bottle of wine, and went out for a walk. That kind of weather wrings me out.

— Me, too.

— I slouched along. I'm afraid I didn't get far. I sat outside a restaurant and drank a lot more wine and ate some chocolate cake. I drank a couple of brandies and sat there in a kind of trance, staring into space. I'm telling you this part because it will explain why I slept until nearly ten o'clock the next morning. Too much booze in that weather, and I'm out. I didn't sleep well, though. Bathed in sweat, hallucinating from the heat and the drink, dreaming every anxiety dream rolled into one. Seeing you had cheered me up temporarily – sort of. I'll get back to that. But now I had the blues. I was never going to find a house in France. It was a stupid, unaffordable idea anyway. Mary doesn't even *like* France. She wanted to move to Ireland, where she claims to have roots. This idea only deepened my shame. Remember, we were supposedly fleeing from a milieu of kids and four-wheel-drive vehicles and skiing holidays and country cottages – the only way you can do that with your chin up is to move to the sunshine. You don't go to Ireland, do you, unless you're utterly defeated?

— That was my understanding, yes.

— This next part is going to be hard for me to tell.

— I'll ask for drinks.

— . . .

— Thanks, Saddler. So. That next morning I dragged myself from bed; I splashed my sunburned face in the sink, was alarmed by how late I had slept and wondered what to do. I could drive on, or I could sneak back your way and hope to find a bargain in your much-more-civilised region. I had loved your house. Perfect gem. And you had told me what it cost. I thought maybe if I struck it lucky with a map or two I might still be able to do the sell-up-and-go routine to a place like yours in your neck of the woods, perhaps without the guest house and stables. I can't believe you aren't able to sell that place.

—I'm forced to ask a price no one is willing to pay. I've had a few . . . setbacks, myself.

— Really? I'm so sorry, how selfish of me to go on this way.

— No, no, carry on. We have plenty of time to get to my little troubles.

— All right. I turned on my radio and it was all about how the elderly French were dying in their thousands from the heat, left in stuffy flats by irresponsible children who had taken the grandkids to the seaside. It was supposed to be shameful. Remember? I was standing there in my room, naked, listening to these stories and wondering if I would rush back from holiday to check on old Gran, if I still had one. Do these people not have telephones? I was sceptical about the news reports. You know how I can be. I reckoned it was just one of nature's culls, and the younger folk are so programmed to get away for a month every summer. Are they supposed to *expect* the heat wave of all time to wipe out their elders? So I went over to the window to get some fresh air of my own. I looked out, and this time I saw that the park wasn't empty. There was a girl lying on her back about forty feet away, sunbathing. Saddler, she was naked.

— Oh dear.

— Well, I froze. It was such a shock – not there being a naked girl sunbathing, but my instant, blinding reaction to the sight. Just in that moment, my head swam, as if I were having a stroke. I'm sure I groaned under my breath. Who knows how long I stood there, reeling, before I caught myself and crouched down below the windowsill. And then I slowly raised myself up, like a scout over the edge of a trench, and scanned the windows opposite. I could see no one. Most of the windows were shuttered up. Then I inched my eyes over the sill and looked back down at the girl. She wasn't reading a book, she wasn't wearing dark glasses. She wasn't wearing anything. She was naked head to foot. She was lying with her back very slightly arched. She had blonde hair that gleamed in the sunlight. She had a long body and long legs, she was smoothly tanned all over. She had breasts like . . . like . . .

— Give us a simile, Hart.

— Oh, like little sand dunes, I suppose. What I mean is small and so delicious I thought I'd faint. That long distance between the middle of her breasts and her . . . her . . .

— Her hips, Hart?

— Yes, yes. I'm not comfortable with that language. The *avenue* down her torso, the slightly whitened *ridges* of her hip bones. I was overwhelmed. No image and no real-life girl ever bowled me over this way. It was her pose, her unexpectedness. And her proximity, though from that distance I couldn't see if, for example, she had freckles, or long eyelashes. I guessed she did.

— And it was hot, and you had a hangover or perhaps were still drunk, and you were naked.

— You're getting the idea.

— Don't be shy, Hart. Not with me.

— I have to tell this accurately, because it may help to explain the way I later behaved. This is going to be hard.

— Oh, I'm sure it *is*.

— Please, Saddler. I slowly stood up. I kept tight against the undrawn curtain. And then a part-dream came over me. You won't believe me. It was so vivid. In the dream part, the erotic fairy tale, I woke her and she seemed to know me, and she smiled. She was perfectly beautiful. In the real world, well, you can imagine, I was quite aroused. I mean, feverish with erection.

— I like this part.

— The thing is – and I don't know how you'll like *this* part – you, Saddler, had something to do with this *Götterdämmerung* of arousal.

— No.

— Possibly. It goes back to my stay at your chateau – and I know it's not a chateau, but I like to think of it that way. I was very pleased to meet your friend Antoine. You'd told me all about him, but we had never met. You had told me he was "the one". You had been together for two years. Is that right?

— Approximately.

— And you'd never felt this way about another man. Never so "domesticated", you said.

— That's true. And it was one of the main reasons we moved to the south of France. So we could get away from the *lifestyle*. The *temptations*. We were starting a life. And so, yes, it follows that he was "the one". Antoine could be the chatelaine, being French, and I could be the mysterious foreigner. It was perfect. I said to myself, "This is the love of my life."

— That's what you told me, too. And I was so pleased to see the way you had arranged it. Antoine is a charming young man, and I was touched by the way he would make excuses to have important things to do, that first evening, so that you and I could talk. I told you this at the time.

— It was a good thing he let us talk, because the next morning the guests descended. Sorry about that.

— I was surprised you wanted families. I knew you liked children, but still.

— Of course I do. These were close friends. I would have had your children stay, and Mary, if you'd brought them along.

— I suppose I should just tell you what I'm getting at. You and I had stayed up until three in the morning, talking about the beginnings of my difficulties, and talking a great deal about how you had found "the one". And the next day a chateau-filling crowd of guests arrived. We had lunch outside. I went to my room and took a nap. Before everyone was supposed to gather for drinks – I don't think I'd even met all the guests by that time – I decided to take a stroll around the grounds.

— You say "grounds". You make it sound like Vaux-le-Viscomte. It's a field and stables with no horses.

— I didn't know there were no horses in the stables at that time. I decided to go and have a look at the horses I thought I might find. I walked down the path by the stream.

— It's an irrigation ditch.

— Fine. As you know, I am no expert on the out-of-doors. For me it was a big step just to be exploring your property. I followed the path down to the stables, ignorant of the flora surrounding me. I'm such an urban creature, if I had seen a squirrel I probably would have fled back to the house. I thought I would see the horses – from a distance, just to say that I'd done so – then walk around the stables to the pool to see if anyone was there. I have to say, the stables were untidy. Weeds, cracked doors, broken windows. And it was through one of these broken windows that I happened to take my first, cautious look.

— For horses.

— Well, I didn't want to confront them face to face. Not right away.

— And what might you have seen when you looked through the broken window?

— I think you probably know what I saw.

— You saw me.

— Yes.

— With someone else.

— Yes.

— Was I chatting with this person?

— No.

— Describe the person, please.

— He was a . . . I was going to say "boy". I *will* say "boy". A blond-haired boy I later learned was your divorced friend Caroline's younger son. I never learned his age.

— All right, if I wasn't chatting with this boy, was I perhaps just standing there, gazing longingly at him?

— No.

— Good for me. I admit it. We were kissing. Sorry to shock you.

— You weren't kissing. You couldn't, the way you were arranged.

— Oh dear.

— Let's say I had a sidelong view.

— And then, of course, you averted your gaze. You ran home as if you'd seen a terrifying squirrel?

— Er . . . No, I'm afraid not. I'm sorry, Saddler, but I was transfixed. I don't mean to embarrass you. There's a point to my telling you this.

— You know very well that I am immune to embarrassment. I've had to be.

— I understand that. The thing is, in all these years – we've known each other three decades, for heaven's sake – you and I have never discussed . . . *details*. I'd always been curious. It's so far outside my own experience. If either of you had seen me, I would have run for it and never mentioned the episode again. What I saw was so extremely passionate, if I may say so. I reeled. I had the feeling I was watching some . . . *apotheosis* in your erotic life.

— You're not far wrong about that. How observant of you.

— Well, in a sense it was a landmark for me, too.

— Oh? Now I'm interested.

— Not in that way. It was more philosophical. I was simply stunned that you had such freedom. To sneak down to your stables with a beautiful young person – you don't have to answer this, but how old was that boy?

— You don't have to call him "that boy". His name is Sam. And he was sixteen at the time.

— Now I'm going to insult you, Saddler. I apologise in advance. But I have to know how such a thing works. I need to know to what extent such a thing can be consensual. What I want to ask you is, did you *pay* Sam?

— The answer to your very rude, inappropriate and inconsiderate question is, "No." Your interest in this matter just shows how naïve you are. I should have taken the time to educate you, over the years. You admit you are ignorant. I'm happy to explain. Sam was inexperienced, but he was not underage. A good-looking fit older man was precisely what he had been after, probably for years. We both knew what was going to happen within half a second of seeing each other that morning in the drive, the first time we'd seen each other since he was a child. I can't make it any plainer than that, unless you want to get into a realm of romance you cannot possibly begin to understand.

— You're right. Except that you're wrong. The only reason I brought up what I saw is because a couple of days later I was looking out of another window, this time at the object of my own desires. What I longed for was completely out of the question, in reality. What you longed for, you got. And am I "naïve" for not seeing the difference? I say to myself, "Out of the question," but in the hotel room at that moment – in fact for several minutes – I was *living* the thing as if it were not only allowed, but possible. Because I had seen you have your way.

— *So* sorry to have whetted your appetite.

— That's what I mean. You did whet my appetite. Nothing would have happened if I hadn't driven away from your place in a state of . . . heightened erotic urge. Really, I have to spell it out. I've nearly had enough to drink to do so, by now. Christ, Saddler, you know what I saw.

— Oh, go on then.

— It wasn't like when I saw the girl in the park, obviously. I'd tell you now if it had been. First I was frightened, then fascinated, then – I mean, Saddler, I'd never seen nor even imagined such a . . . such a *brutal* scene. I could clearly see the boy's – Sam's – face. There were moments when he might have spotted me if he'd opened his eyes. I'd only encountered this sort of thing in literature, and I always found it unbelievable. Yet there it was before my eyes. And you know what it was that really turned me on, in the end? I think it was the illicitness, plus the freedom you had. That, and a pair of male orgasms the likes of which I know for a fact I have never experienced in my life. You guys came like locomotives, my friend. Only then did I sneak away. I can't believe you didn't notice the state I was in, at dinner that evening.

— In fact I do remember thinking you were grumpy about something. I thought you resented my other guests. I thought you wanted me to yourself.

— Well, imagine if you'd wandered down to the stables and found me rogering a sixteen-year-old – hang on, don't answer that. It's part of my point. Of course, that would be unthinkable.

— So, you were angry because you disapproved, or because you were envious?

— Both, I suppose.

— It isn't like you to moralise. You were always the libertine, or you said you were.

— I said I *wanted* to be. I guess it didn't work out that way. That sort of thing has to be in your character. It was easier for you, I think. No matter what you say, no matter how things have changed, you're still by definition an outlaw, no matter what the legislation says. And I think you like it that way.

— I'll have to think about that, Hart. But for the sake of this argument, I won't deny what you say is true.

— I'll tell you the real reason I was angry. You'll think I'm wet, but it boggled my mind that you would betray Antoine that way.

Sorry. You said he was "the one". Call me romantic. He was so charming. He loved you, quite obviously. And so, putting aside all of the qualms I might have had about what you were doing, the main thing was that I thought you were being unfaithful to good old Antoine, who seemed to be making such an effort. I thought that was cruel.

— Hmm.

— And what became of Antoine, may I ask?

— He ran away with a mutual friend and broke my heart.

— I'm sorry, Saddler.

— You won't believe me, after what you saw, but I really made a go of it with Antoine. How can you not love someone who dresses only in white? God, he was beautiful. I have to fake being stylish. Antoine was *sui generis*. He turned affectedness on its head.

— You looked good together.

— Thank you. He is now living in Dubrovnik with a fat sixty-year-old Italian hotel-chain heir. Gold-digging little whore Antoine turned out to be.

— That must take some of the sting out of it.

— Indeed it does. Anyway, you left my house the next day, in a huff.

— Yes. And I did my half-hearted property hunting. And I did my drinking in the heat. And I awoke late to see the girl who changed my life, lying naked in the little park. I can't tell you how different this was from the usual pangs one feels when a pretty girl walks by in the street. This was the powerful, swooning, nauseating feeling of falling in love. I saw the full scenario, how I would wait for her to get up, follow her into the town, contrive an introduction. She would smile adorably and take my arm. Then coffee, a light meal, the tension building and building. Back to my room in a breathless rush through the narrow streets, holding hands. Her slender arms around my neck, et cetera. I was deranged, Saddler. I was a quivering, fantasising, maniacal sex-zombie after only a few minutes that had already been prolonged in my imagination to a day and a night.

— And you were holding your cock in your hand.

— Yes, thank you. Feel free to add the words I'm too bashful to say. That is exactly what I was holding in my hand. And then I began to . . .

— Make love to yourself?

— Well put. And I took my time, Saddler. I remember expecting the girl to move, in response to my touch. I don't want to tell you the next part, but it's important. When I was . . . finishing—

— Coming.

— Thank you, yes. Well, I was pressing my head against the window frame—

— As one does.

— Then against the windowpane itself. And I had no regard for anything so I simply . . .

— Ejaculated.

— Yes, on the windowsill. Copiously, as you can well imagine.

— I'm trying, Hart.

— My knees buckled. I fell back onto the bed. I hugged one of the pillows to my chest and face. I kissed the pillow. I spoke to the pillow. I told the pillow I loved it. I believe I was having a *petit mort*. Then I fell asleep.

— What a very happy, relaxing experience. I'm guessing that was not the end of your morning's excitement, though.

— I don't think I'd been asleep for more than twenty minutes before they burst into my room. There were three of them, two men and a woman, and the cleaning lady behind them in the corridor with a key in her hand. This was a very small room, and the three people filled it. I lurched upright on the bed, with the pillow in my lap. I was pouring sweat. I hadn't shaved since the day before I left your place. I stood up at the side of the bed near the window, still covering myself with the pillow. I backed up against the wall to where I'd been standing before I collapsed. I demanded to know who the people were and what they wanted, and before they replied I told them all to get the hell out of my room. One of them, Saddler, was a policeman. The other man was the hotel manager. The woman was elderly, white hair full of pins, and she wore a ragged pink terry-cloth robe and matching slippers. I realised I had been speaking – or even shouting, in my alarm – in English. "What's going on here?" the policeman asked me, in French. "That's what I want to know." At this point, because I was coming to my senses and had a vague idea what the problem might be, I glanced out of the window to my left. There were several people there now, and the girl was motionless on the ground. Several things occurred to me on the spot. Why would a girl be sunbathing completely naked in a public place when the sun had hardly cleared the rooftops? Why had there been no possessions nor clothing at her side? Why was she lying on the dry grass instead of on a blanket or a towel? Why had she not moved a muscle during the minutes I had watched her? And most of all, why the hell had I not noticed any of these things? I turned back to the people in my room and blinked at them. Again, I asked them what was going on, even though I thought I knew. They weren't looking at me, this time. They were looking at the windowsill.

— Oh, no.

— Saddler, that girl was dead.

— Christ.

— And the woman in the robe had seen me from her kitchen window on the other side of the courtyard, doing what I had been doing. And there was one more little detail I didn't want to hear.

— What's that, then?

— She was twelve years old.

— Oh, hell.

— I just want to say I think it does me good to tell you this.

— My God, though. What an ordeal.

— It was only beginning. The young, inexperienced gendarme

radioed for backup and wouldn't even let me dress. He told me to stay where I was. I had a good view of what they were doing to the girl's body, which was covering it with a sheet and keeping people away from the crime scene. The old woman left my room in tears. The hotel manager stayed, as if it would take both men to stop me if I went fleeing, naked, into the streets. You can just imagine what I looked like to them. Hair plastered to scalp with sweat, sunburned face unshaven, naked body white, wine bottle empty on bedside table, own seed *splashed* about the place. They had a witness to my perversity, my deviance. They had a dead girl in the quad. It was obvious what they thought they had here, cowering in the corner of the room: a paedophile necrophilliac.

— Bad luck, Hart.

— The policeman and the manager whispered to each other. I stood leaning back against the wall, the pillow covering my shameful loins. Over my shoulder, I watched a small crowd gathering around the body of the dead girl. A detective entered the room about five minutes later, an extraordinary-looking man. He had a great, handsome head that would have suited a tall man but which was attached to a tiny body – spidery legs, a child's feet, no hips, practically no torso. He wore the uniform: black leather jacket over white T-shirt, stovepipe jeans, black running shoes. By the time the detective arrived, that hotel room and the scene just outside had become my whole world. My thoughts raced. I could hardly make eye contact with the odd-looking figure in the leather jacket. I was very slightly relieved when the first thing he said was directed at the young policeman: "For God's sake, you couldn't have let him put his clothes on?" I took this sympathetic remark as my cue, and sidled around the bed to a wooden chair where I had laid my clothes the night before. The three men averted their gazes as I dressed. The detective asked me to come with him, and gave the copper instructions to seal my room until he returned. Now, this detective – whose name was

Claude Cambon – was so relaxed that his insect body seemed to melt into the car seat. He hadn't arrested me, he hadn't handcuffed me, he only asked me to go with him. He drove me to the police station next door to the Hôtel de Ville. He said he was going to make me wait, but not long. He was the kind of detective who needed to do his investigating first, his interrogation later. He had a surprising, booming voice coming out of that oversized head. And he was ridiculously nonchalant. How many dead girls could have turned up in the middle of his small town? He seemed to treat this catastrophe as an inconvenience. He didn't put me in a cell. Without having asked me a single question, he told me to wait in an unlocked room with a sofa and coffee table. "I'll have someone bring you a coffee," he said. Then he was off, to hook up with his man from forensics. Have you ever been detained by the police, Saddler?

— Never.

— Well I don't know about you, but like a lot of people I irrationally panic every time I see a policeman in the street. I always imagine I'm carrying a kilo of heroin, when I'm not. So now that it was happening in reality – it took a while for all of this to seem real, actually – my brain began to fizz with dread. I was certain I was guilty of whatever crime Cambon would eventually accuse me of having committed. When a woman brought me the coffee I clattered the cup in its saucer.

— Still, you knew you'd done nothing wrong.

— Nothing wrong? For starters I'd committed an obscene act in public, or publicly enough for at least one person to have seen me. Other possibilities crossed my mind – I was alone in that room for about two hours, so I had plenty of time to think. The old woman must have seen me wanking away while watching a dead girl.

— You didn't know she was dead.

— Cambon certainly didn't see it that way. When he returned he was ruffled. I imagine he'd had to get down on his hands and knees and examine the girl's body. He probably had to tell the parents – it turns out they were from out of town, staying in a fancy hotel in the town centre. He sat down right next to me on the sofa. I didn't know if my French would be up to an interrogation. The detective flipped open a small notebook and began to ask me the basics. You'd think he would have wanted his interview on tape, and because he merely jotted down my replies I took this as a good sign. I was so nervous I could hardly remember my own address. We managed to get through the preliminaries, and then he asked me if I knew the dead girl. I said I didn't know her. Cambon nodded his big head, very gravely. The next thing I knew I'd been "held for further questioning" and put in a jail cell. Cambon left. No one would explain anything to me. I had no idea what kind of rights I had. A telephone call? I would probably have called you, Saddler, if they'd given me the chance. Later on they did, but by that time I'd decided to ride the thing out and tell no one.

— Not even Mary?

— Especially not Mary.

— But that's mad.

— That's easy to say now. You can't imagine how terrified I was.

— I believe you.

— Someone checked me out of the hotel, packed up my suitcase. I spent the night in the cell – it didn't have bars or anything. It was almost like my hotel room, in fact. I was taken to a canteen to eat. There was only one other prisoner being held, a well-dressed man about my age whom they'd accused of abusing his wife by spitting at her repeatedly in a bank queue. He was unapologetic and philosophical. He asked me why I was being held, and I said they thought I was a murdering paedophile necrophilliac, but that I wasn't, not really. He didn't speak to me again after that, and I doubt he slept well during the night. You're looking a little pale, Saddler.

— I'm not sure if you're telling the truth. At least you're exaggerating.

— I swear to God.

— And you've told no one?

— Not until now. That doesn't mean some people haven't found out, over time.

— The murder – I'm assuming the girl was murdered, at a minimum – must have got into the newspapers.

— Oh, she was murdered, all right. And the story did make the papers. Only locally, thank God. Remember, this happened when many thousands were dying all over France, from the heat wave. If it made national news, I never read it. If it made radio, I never heard it. If it made television, I never saw it. Best to have one's paedophile necrophillia occur during a crowded news cycle.

— You're not going to tell me you were charged?

— Well. I awoke – yes, I was able to sleep, unlike my expectorating roommate – and Cambon took me out to a café for breakfast. Can you believe it? My head had cleared enough for this gesture to make me suspicious. Wasn't there formal procedure, even in the French countryside? If Cambon believed I was involved in the murder of a twelve-year-old girl, why was he buying me coffee and a *pain aux raisins* in broad daylight? At first he seemed only to want to talk about another case. He was completely relaxed, and this relaxed me. I see now that he did that deliberately. He told me about a woman he suspected of having murdered her husband, whose body had never been found during the two years since his disappearance. She worked in one of the town's three *tabacs*, and since her husband vanished she had set up home with her female partner. The detective had tried everything to trick his suspect into a false move or a confession. She was imperturbable. "She seems happy now," Cambon said, shrugging his shoulders. "But I hate failure." As a segue into the case at hand, Cambon told me he had a twelve-year-old daughter. He described her – small for her age, bookish, sweet and serene – and then he said, "I wanted to tell you this, because if I seem a little . . . distanced right now, it's not because I'm insensitive. It is because I am trying to hide my feelings. This is the greatest tragedy of my career, and I'm still coming to grips with it. I'll forget about the lesbian. I will not rest until this new case is solved. And so I need to speak to you." I told him I understood that. I also said that I'd seen absolutely nothing that could be of any help to him. It seemed natural for me to say that. We were chatting like friends.

— Smooth fellow, your Cambon.

— I didn't see anything coming. "So, you didn't know Annette?" Without thinking I said, "No, I didn't know her." "Then how did you know her name?" "Oh, wait. I didn't mean I didn't know *Annette*, I just assumed you meant the poor girl." "So you did know Annette?" "No, no . . ." It went on this way for a while until I thought Cambon understood me when I said I didn't know the dead girl. "So you never saw her before." "That's right." Then Cambon took a sip of coffee, smacked his lips and said, "I have information that says otherwise."

— If I may interrupt for a second, Hart?

— Go ahead.

— This is exactly the sixth moment you've described when I would have demanded to have a lawyer present. Did this not occur to you?

— Not for a minute. That was Cambon's trick. He took me out to breakfast, for heaven's sake. This was no third degree, or at least it didn't feel like one at the time. He took me in. He was shaking hands with people as they came into the café and introducing me as "my English friend". So, no, having a lawyer present did not occur to me.

— What, then, was your detective's information?

— He told me about going to see the dead girl's parents at their hotel. They had reported her missing at about one o'clock in the morning. The father had already been out scouring the streets. They said she – Annette – had gone out for an ice cream at about eleven o'clock. They saw no problem with letting her do this on her own. It was a well-lit part of town, plenty of people still out late at this time of year. Cambon told me the whole thing – still softening me up, keeping me off my guard, I now realise. It was almost as if he were showing off his skills, and wanted to include his "English friend" in the investigation that he didn't doubt would exonerate me. He didn't mind when I asked questions. He described Annette's parents as Parisians on holiday, well heeled, the father a property man – a bit like you, Saddler. The father fixed up houses in the Auvergne, and sold them to rain-weary Belgians. He and his wife were understandably frantic. Cambon stayed up with them all night. No one had seen her, not even the ice cream man. Annette was fairly independent, they said – she walked a kilometre each way to school and back in Paris every day – but she had never deviated from any agreed plan. She looked older than her age – don't I know it – and they said she was mature. Cambon told me all of this, and answered any questions I had about his search during the night, and then he lowered the boom. He said he'd gone back to my hotel and found my passport, made a photocopy, and brought my picture to show to Annette's parents. They recognised me straightaway. "The man in the restaurant," they said. They remembered me very well. They said they thought I had been staring at Annette. They recalled everything vividly. They remembered that I looked "like a vagrant", and that I wasn't eating in the restaurant, only drinking. They said I had a frightening look on my face, and after a while they arranged their chairs so that they had their backs to me. They particularly stated that I wouldn't take my eyes off Annette, and I had made her uncomfortable. The father told Cambon he'd had half a mind to confront me, or at least to complain to the waiter.

— Do you remember any of that?

— Actually, I do. I wouldn't have recognised the girl in the restaurant if I saw her again, but I do remember being in that hypnotised state I already described to you, and feeling drunk and washed out from the booze and the terrible heat. I think I recall saying to myself that the girl in the hat – the girl in the restaurant wore a floppy white hat – must have thought I was staring at her, when in fact I was staring way, way into the distance behind her. I was practically asleep. As for looking like a "vagrant", well, that's just Parisian talk for someone unshaven and sweaty.

— Did you tell this to Cambon?

— Not right away. I should have. I wasn't really clear in my own mind what I'd done or not done at that restaurant, and for the moment I didn't want to take the parents' word for my behaviour. So I said I'd gone to that restaurant, had a drink and some chocolate cake, and that I didn't remember a girl, much less staring at one.

— I'm betting Cambon had already spoken to your waiter.

— Yes. The waiter reported that I drank a whole bottle of wine and two brandies with my cake. He remembered that I was unshaven and sweaty. As for my staring at the girl, he hadn't noticed if I had, but wouldn't have been surprised because I was drunk.

— Were you? Drunk, I mean.

— Oh, I suppose so, yes, of course. But as I told you, it was more as if I'd gone into a trance. It's easy in hindsight to blame the heat and the fatigue, but I stand by that excuse for my behaviour. I told Cambon that if the girl's parents said I was making their daughter uncomfortable, they were probably right. Who was I to call them liars? I thought I was being very suave, taking this insouciant line. I was implying, "Maybe I was staring at the girl – what of it?"

— I take it this approach backfired?

— Cambon chewed on a toothpick and looked very pleased with himself, as if he were halfway to my full confession. He kept rubbing his neck. That big head of his on such a skinny stalk. And he looked exhausted. He'd been up two nights. But still he smiled at my admission that I had been staring at the girl in the restaurant. Then he actually laughed when I asked him, in all seriousness, if he had a suspect for the murder. I didn't know if they had been able to gather any evidence at the scene, and of course I knew that even if they had, none of it could possibly point to me.

— I see. All they had was a drunk, ogling vagrant who was found masturbating in the proximity of a dead girl.

— That's one way of looking at it. I have to tell you, having thought about this for a long time, that I think I actually enjoyed this informal interrogation. As it was happening, mind you, not later on. It was perverse. I think I liked the attention of being a murder suspect. With all my troubles at home, here I was in a foreign land, and I was not going unnoticed. I'd made a splash in old St-Vuis. I was getting a free breakfast. I even had the thought – and here is where I truly *fucked* myself – that there might be a way to get some money out of the situation I found myself in. Can you believe it? The madness? I honestly, consciously thought that if I strung Cambon along, brought my story right to the fringe of guilt, I could parlay my total innocence into a lawsuit – or at any rate compensation of some kind. I might find myself on the telly. That was my line of thinking, I swear.

— You had lost your mind.

— Obviously. But this madness lasted only the morning. In the afternoon things got darker. I was put back in the holding room while Cambon went about his investigation, and I began to think about what I'd done. Not what Cambon wanted to accuse me of doing, but what I had *actually done*. The phrase I've used, "paedophile necrophilliac". Now, isn't that what I was, in fact?

— Though not a *murdering* paedophile necrophilliac – from what you've told me as yet.

— No. But my actions were those of a sad twisted pervert, and I began to feel guilty. I started to think, what kind of sick bastard *am* I?

— I'm not sure I like your tone here, Hart. You seem to have been worried about yourself when you were caught up in a tragedy. That poor girl, her poor parents – what a nightmare.

— I know, and I'm sorry. I don't mean to be flip about any of this, but it's the only self-defence I have. Even now, after all this time, it still doesn't seem real. I see it all through a heat haze. You know how I am, Saddler. In any crisis I go all calm and fatalistic. It's not only selfishness. I can look at a situation, as I did in France, and my reaction is to strike off things I can't do anything about.

— A dead girl, for example.

— Exactly. Part of it was shock, part was embarrassment, but in the end self-preservation was paramount. That, I thought I could control. And I thought I could prevent Mary from finding out. I mean, she might already have thought I was a wanker, but to be, *literally*, a wanker . . .

— Speaking of your wife, I ran into Bea Cook yesterday – Mary's chum? I hadn't seen her in about six years, not entirely accidentally. She went out of her way during a short conversation – we just bumped into each other in the street outside my flat – to say that your Mary was "transformed". I asked what she meant by this, and she said Mary had been "slimming", that she was "absolutely wasting away" – and she meant this as a compliment, I believe. Could this so-called transformation be related to your problems, Hart?

— Oh, God, I hope not. No, no. Bea's crazy. This is a separate issue, but still very worrying. I don't know how to speak to Mary about it. Saddler, I think she's bulimic, or one of those things. Her friends only reinforce it. A great worry. I'm afraid to say anything to her about it. She's not quite skeletal but getting there. Mood-wise, her ups and downs are more frequent than they were. There is a slight chance that she found out about what I got up to in France – I'll get to the reasons why I suspect she did. At first I thought she would definitely have confronted me if she had. I hate all the psychological nonsense – she can do what she wants, that's what I maintain – but some might say that, with our declining fortunes, her becoming extremely slim was a way of putting one over on her increasingly well-fed contemporaries, and she's taken the project too far. I don't know . . . Anyway, it's not about what she may or may not know about France. And what about you? You were in the country at the time – and since – and you never heard a peep. Right?

— I have a vague recollection of the girl's death. There are so many, though. I don't think it caught the public's imagination.

— That's because there was no rape.

— Wasn't there?

— Cambon was good enough to share that information with me at our breakfast. The forensic chaps were able to determine this at the scene. Annette, it turns out, was a virgin.

— I didn't know detectives were supposed to be so free with their inside dope.

— That's Cambon's style. He was still trying to make me think I was nothing more than a witness who might be of some help, that I was assisting him with his investigation. He kept asking me, over and over, if I could remember having seen anything during the night or early in the morning. Did I happen to get up to use the toilet and look out of the window? What was the first thing I noticed about the scene when I finally got up? I stupidly pretended to try to think of something I might have seen, when the truth was so simple and humiliating. What I couldn't see was that Cambon was gearing up to ask me if I'd followed Annette's family from the restaurant, loitered in the street, seen her come out alone, dragged her into an alley, marched her to my hotel, killed her and left her body on the grass, returned to my room and had my way with myself while looking at her. He frequently digressed. He told me about his wife, a nursery school teacher originally from Nantes. He mentioned his daughter again, to emphasise his sympathy for Annette's parents. "I've never had to do that before," he told me, meaning having to break such cataclysmic news. There had been a kidnapping a few years ago, he said, when the parents of an eight-year-old girl had to wait sixteen months before the body was discovered, hundreds of miles away. Cambon said that Annette's parents were relatively lucky to have had their ordeal compressed into a single night and half a morning. I asked him about Annette's parents, and that was the first time he stiffened and hesitated in replying. It was also the first time I was aware of feeling like a suspect rather than a witness or a minor sexual miscreant. Cambon could play his game with me, but only up to a point. He was uncomfortable talking about Annette's parents with the only person he could so far connect with the dead girl, and in a sordid way at that. But he did volunteer that the father, Vincent Fastin, had been more hysterical than his wife, Marie-Laure, who sat down and sobbed into a hotel bath towel and didn't look up for half an hour. Vincent, who had been out in the town's streets all night long searching for his daughter, flew into a rage. Cambon said this was not how he'd heard fathers normally reacted. They tended to go numb, to get a vacant look in their eyes, to let their masculine brains wrestle with the impossibility of rewinding time. Obviously, he blamed himself for letting Annette go outside alone at a late hour. Cambon tried to calm him down, but eventually summoned a doctor to give him a jab.

— Did the father ask about you?

— Indeed he did. In the sense of wanting to know where I was, so that he could kill me with his bare hands. He said he wanted to strangle me with my own entrails.

— Did Vincent know you had been detained, and why?

— Cambon said no, but I think he was lying. I think he told Vincent he'd picked me up and I was safely behind bars. It would have been something if Vincent had wandered into that café and seen me chatting with the detective as if we were old friends. His hotel was right around the corner.

— So you weren't charged, but he put you back in the holding room? On what grounds?

— Probably on the grounds that I didn't protest. I was only there a few hours that day. After lunch, Cambon came in and said I was free to go, but that he wanted me to stay in St-Vuis until he gave me permission to continue on my way. He advised me to change hotels and to stay inside, as Vincent had made a direct threat on my life. So that is what I did, looking over my shoulder the whole time.

— And at that point you began in earnest not to ring your wife.

— That's not true. I rang her every day. I told her I'd seen a house with possibilities. I described the house with the library, making it sound far better than it was. I said there was room for a swimming pool, that sort of thing. I said the old man who owned it was almost literally dying to sell. I said I had a second appointment to see it, which had been cancelled. It was extremely strange to be lying outright to Mary. I had rarely needed to before.

— And she sounded unconcerned?

— Yes. She sounded normal, even interested in France, for a change. Anyway, once I was installed I could see that Cambon had stationed a man across the street from my hotel. This was presumably both to make sure I stayed put, and at the same time to protect me from the vengeful, grieving Vincent. Cambon kept me abreast of his investigation. I sneaked out once a day, for three days, for food supplies – and for the local newspaper, to follow the media version of Annette's murder. The police were said to be following important leads, but couldn't comment any further. They had no one in custody, but had interviewed important witnesses. From what I could tell, the story really wasn't catching fire. I don't know how I passed the time, other than rolling around in my own sweat, unable to sleep. I felt sick with shame. Finally Cambon told me I could leave. He had no evidence against me, he said. I asked him if he had evidence against anyone else, and he shook his big head. "But don't tell anyone," he said. We shook hands. I thought I'd never see him again.

— I can't believe you didn't come straight back to my house, or that you didn't just pick up the telephone and tell me what was happening.

— My plan was to make the whole nightmare go away. It looked possible. I would stew in my own disgrace but keep it to myself. I got into my car, turned up the air conditioning, and drove non-stop home, where I could face the future and spend my time lying by omission.

— I think this fellow Cambon treated you very well. He didn't feed you to the press. He let you out of jail the moment he could. You were unlucky, but you didn't do anything anyone else wouldn't have done under the circumstances.

— I tried to look at it that way. But there's no denying the guilt. I felt so terrible, I simply assumed I must have done something very wrong.

— If the old woman hadn't seen you, and if the girl hadn't turned out coincidentally to be . . . well, *dead*, you would have put the episode out of your mind.

— Perhaps. You're right that what I did was not technically illegal or even "wrong". Harmless, human – tender, even. But what you got up to with Sam, that was technically not illegal, but what if you'd been caught by someone other than me? Someone who told Sam's parents, for example. What if they found out?

— Ah, but they did.

— What?

— Oh yes. She didn't quite get your view, Hart, but Sam's mother caught us together the next day, after you'd left. We were in Sam's bedroom that time.

— Jesus. You couldn't have thought to lock the door?

— The door was locked, all right. It would have been better if it hadn't been. We had just finished dressing. She knocked. We froze. "I know you're in there!" When I opened the door, all smiles, Sam's face said it all to her. Caroline was an old friend, Hart. What I'd done was the worst thing that had ever happened to her in her life. Unlike you, I couldn't make it disappear. She desperately wanted to keep it secret, but she cracked within days and then everyone knew. I was ostracised. And, of course, she made sure Antoine knew. It was very unpleasant, and it made me rethink my whole attitude towards love. I should probably add that I was Sam's godfather.

— Dear me.

— It was excruciating all round.

— So. We are still trying to argue that we both did nothing "wrong", and yet we feel terrible.

— In the long run it sounds as if I got off worse than you did. I lost a lot of friends. You seem to be in the clear.

— Saddler, that's where you're wrong. But I'm sorry to have gone on so long about my difficulties. I had no idea what you'd been through.

— The gentlemanly thing for me to say would be that it was worse for Sam.

— Have you seen him since?

— Well . . . Because you've been so candid about your own behaviour, the answer to your question is yes. He's almost eighteen now. He's a light-hearted person. He lives as a just-passing straight boy at university. He's shy, and he dislikes what he calls the "pretentious" scene. He's here in London, and I've seen him five times in as many months. I get news about my former friends from him. They think I'm a monster. Perhaps I am. That's where I stand at the moment. My business has gone to hell, given that I tended to sell property through a network of friends. Know anyone who needs a house with empty stables in the south of France? My own crowd won't come near me.

— I'll certainly ask around. Not that my circle – that is to say, Mary's circle – don't already have their bloody places abroad. Imagine a world where the London house, the country cottage and a great farmhouse on the Continent are the norm. It's galling. The only thing to do is turn one's back. Mary wants to compete. She hasn't given up. She looks to me to find a way.

— From what you've said, you're fucked.

— I have my delusional plans. I've thought of just about every scheme I could conjure up during sleepless nights. I do have a job, at the moment, which I keep quiet about. I'm a consultant to a broker. Right up my street. Pacific maps, Middle Ages euro-maps. He's got a lot on his plate, and he sends me out into the world to value the minor items while he deals in the great rarities. I earn enough to keep the car running, basically, for trips to my accountant and back. This is not a long-term solution. The wolf is well and truly salivating in my vestibule.

— At least it's something. You can get back in the game, I'm sure of it.

— Possibly. I'll get to that. But in the meantime there have been developments. I spent the first six months after I got home from France just ticking off the days that I wasn't busted. Mary didn't appear to suspect a thing. She had her own worries. I got not the slightest hint that anyone knew what had happened to me, that I had briefly been a murder suspect. This isn't to say I wasn't uneasy, not to say paranoid. For weeks I thought I was being followed. And then I realised I *was* being followed. I swear it's true. For at least four days I saw the same man, always after dark, lurking in the shadows near my house or ducking into a shop in the street where I occasionally have to visit my employer. The first telephone call reached me in the New Year. A man, English, speaking *faux* Estuary. He identified himself as "a concerned observer". I hardly said a word to him. I didn't react. He didn't say much, either. He said, "I'm trying to decide what to do about you, Mr Hart." The next time he called, a week later, he said, "Does St-Vuis seem a long time ago, Mr Hart?" He pronounced it "Saint *Voo*iss".

— And so you confessed everything to Mary, to cut your losses?

— I did not. I still didn't know what the man knew. I didn't know what he wanted from me. I found that out a few days later. He called me again – he always called me on my mobile, always when I was alone. He said he had a close friend in Fleet Street – he used that term – who would be interested in the Saint *Voo*iss story.

— Had you been in touch with Detective Cambon?

— Several times. I thought it behoved me to get in touch now and then, to show I hadn't run away, that I wasn't avoiding him, that mine was an innocent man's curiosity in a tragedy that had touched my life. Cambon had no leads whatsoever, certainly nothing further that pointed at me.

— Did your caller give a name?

— No. He made it clear, over a period of weeks, that he knew I had been detained in St-Vuis after the murder of a Parisian girl. He knew some details. He knew about what I'd been seen doing at the window.

— I never asked you, Hart, how the girl was killed. I just assumed she was strangled.

— You were right. That's one thing Cambon wouldn't get specific about. He wouldn't tell me what she was strangled with. And there's a perfect example of how I screwed up during my breakfast interview with him. I made the same assumption you did, that Annette had been strangled. And during our conversation I asked if it had been a rope or a tie or something else.

— Before he'd told you she'd been strangled.

— Correct. One more box to be checked in Cambon's detective mind. I went so far as to ask Cambon if ever, in his fairly long career, he'd heard of a young girl being strangled, left naked in the open and so on, without having been raped first. I asked him this question outright: "Who would kill such a beautiful young girl without raping her first?" You can imagine the silence.

— So your mystery caller knew all or most of this. And you immediately called the police.

— Er . . . no.

— You're starting to frustrate me.

— Here was my line of thought: plenty of St-Vuis locals must have known about Cambon's "English friend" having been under a kind of house arrest for a few days after Annette's murder. Probably everyone sitting in the café where we'd met for breakfast would have found out right away who I was, where I was from, what I was suspected of having done. The woman at the hotel must certainly have blabbed to anyone who'd listen about the filthy pervert across the way. There were loads of tourists about who might have got wind of the story. One or more of these people could have found out my name, either directly from Cambon – though I doubt it – or from the police, the hotel manager, the gendarme, the old lady. They knew I was English. They could have located me with ease. And, of course, the girl's parents themselves could have tipped off the caller – they'd seen my passport. To what end, I had no idea. Also weighing heavily on my mind was that Mary knew where I had been.

— Blackmail would have been my first instinct.

— Which is what it was, at the beginning.

— I have to ask again. Why didn't you simply confess all to Mary, get it off your chest and ignore these jokers?

— In a word, the climate.

— The climate?

— The social climate. The obsession with child abuse.

— It's not as if you're a schoolteacher, Hart.

— It makes no difference. I was exposed, as it were. I had my new job. I'd be tainted as at the very least a potential child molester.

— Unlike an actual one, like me.

— I don't know about that, Saddler. What I know is that it's not as if I were an MP or an actor or someone people vaguely cared about, but I was convinced that any small explosion would put an end to whatever I still clung to.

— You thought you'd lose your job?

— And my wife. And my children. That is how I thought at the time. I was willing to do anything.

— Where are you working, then?

— My boss, for about a year now, is called Rory Fine – know of him?

— I don't think so.

— Our paths had crossed over the years. I'd known his wife first, rather well. Rory's infuriating. He's one of those men who will announce, after dinner, after everyone else has bitched about their problems, that he's casually set up a little shop in Bloomsbury and thinks he might shift a manuscript or two. So you drop by and there he is, with a staff of eight in three plush storeys, a guard at the front door, exhibits behind bullet-proof glass, a receptionist who looks like bloody Cleopatra, humidified palm trees pressing their fronds to the ceiling, Persian carpets, secret oak doors leading to secret viewing rooms, a bachelor pad on the top floor, cabinets groaning with impeccably organised treasures, exquisite lighting throughout, champagne and hors d'oeuvres for all comers, and fat Rory in the middle of it all with a red face, big belly and subtle kilt. I always wonder how the world throws up such dynamos.

— They work harder than we do.

— It isn't work for Rory. I've known him twenty years, and he's always been that way. It's like breathing to him. He does more before breakfast than I can do . . . in a lifetime, really. And he's not even wealthy and never has been. He doesn't need to be. He loves his business; he has a delightful wife, three sons, at least one bubbly young mistress I know of. His life is perfect. I always thought you had to be rich to get the things you wanted, but no. Rory Fine has *nailed* it. That's why he's infuriating.

— Well, good for him. That's the way he likes it. Some of us have different constitutions. You and I are more contemplative, perhaps.

— It was kind of him to hire me. As well as humiliating, naturally.

— You work on commission?

— Yes. I get an upfront finder's fee until Rory makes his sale, then I get a cut. I think he's getting impatient with me because in the last six months I've found nothing but garbage. I don't earn enough to pay my blackmailer, never mind school fees. This is why I've . . . cheated.

— You? You cheated?

— Watch me turn scarlet as I confess this to you, Saddler. You're the only person I could possibly, *possibly* tell. I'm not terribly proud of any of this.

— I wouldn't speak to a soul.

— I have at least two more confessions to make before I ask for your advice, and your help. I have to digress here for a moment because, Saddler, your very first instinct about what I was going to tell you today was right, in that it's a part of all the strange things that have happened to me since we last saw each other.

— At last it comes out. You're having an affair, Hart.

— Yes and no.

— For God's sake. Have you put it where it doesn't belong or not?

— I wouldn't say *that*. Seems to belong just fine. Give me a chance here. I'm exposing myself to you.

— If only.

— Now, just listen to me. I find this extraordinary. And stop looking at your watch; I'll let you go soon.

— Don't worry. I've freed up the whole day for you.

— All right. This happened between the blackmail and the cheating, if you follow.

— That would be, what, six months ago?

— Yes. My nerves were raw; I wandered about feeling awkward, guilty, plotless. The tension on the home front had been building roughly since the day we were married, as I understand is normal, that is to say twelve fucking years. I told myself the only problem was money. Well, the problem *was* money. You know how I adore Mary.

— So you keep insisting.

— Well, for quite a long time she had begun to stress my responsibility for her upkeep, a duty I would gladly have taken on if I *could* have. She had such expectations. We *had* to do this, we *had* to do that, and all of these things we *had* to do cost money I didn't have but *had* to get hold of pronto. Ski trips, for example. Imagine a world in which ski trips are compulsory. Imagine spending a week with a two-year-old on skis falling around between your legs while your pregnant wife reads Indian novels on the chalet sun terrace.

— I'm trying. Funnily enough, I can't.

— I bring up skiing because of the way Mary and I met.

— I can recite it for you as if I lived it myself, Hart.

— I know, I know. But I just couldn't help comparing those early ski trips – first lift to the top of the glacier, cold beer and ham, sex all afternoon, cocktails, dinner, dancing – with the humiliating chore of skiing *en famille*. The first time I laid eyes on Mary was as I walked along one of those sun terraces. There were a lot more pretty girls in those days, it seems to me, and she was the prettiest. She and her gang.

— Chalet girls, Hart. She was a chalet girl.

— And why not? Who the hell are you to sneer at that? She loved skiing, the job paid her way.

— I don't mean to sneer. Just the reputation.

— Do you mean the gold-digging reputation, like your *Antoine*, or the hooker reputation, or the dizzy no-A-level hooker gold-digger reputation? It was love. You know I wasn't exactly at a loose end in that regard.

— The girls always loved you, Hart. They sensed the danger in your cruel icy blues.

— So, let a dozen years pass. Blameless years in at least one major sense.

— Really?

— Mostly. The skiing had become an unaffordable, exhausting annual grind of joyless labour . . . Oh, never mind the skiing. It's an example of the unaffordable, exhausting, grind of joyless labour life had become, and before you bark at me that I am not alone in living this cliché, I am *aware* of that. And then, six months ago, still bruised and haunted by the Annette imbroglio, a young French woman who might have *been* Annette if you added ten years to her age, walked up to me and introduced herself.

— What, like that? In the street?

— No, at an awful party. It was a charity benefit that one of Mary's wealthy friends invited us to, a most blatant stab to my ribs because everyone else would carelessly be bidding on plasma televisions or trips to the Maldives and I'd be standing there, hands deep in empty pockets. This is one of the ways Mary's friends try to get back at her for being so pretty and slim. They hold me up, dangle me in the glare of their husbands' sickening rise to financial wholeness. Mary cheered on the bidders, drank a great deal of champagne and ignored me. I kept my head down in the shadows, behind the throng, and didn't even glance in the direction of the famous MC. That's when the girl approached me. I thought, Jesus, she works for these people and she's going to order me to get my wallet out for the earthquake victims, or whatever cause we were benefiting by getting drunk and buying first-class holidays. "Oh," said this girl. "I'm sorry, I thought I recognised you." That's good, isn't it?

— I like it.

— This will seem very convoluted and time-wasting to someone like you, Saddler, but people like me don't just dash down into the stables to—

— Enough of that. Watch your step. Apples and oranges. You're out of line. You're insulting me.

— I'm sorry. Please, I'm very sorry, Saddler.

— OK. Just don't bring me into this anymore than you have to. You're sweating guilt already, and taking it out on me. Unjustly.

— Sorry. So, the young woman, who spoke perfect English, was the kind of person who presses up to one, and in three minutes she had me babbling the way I'm doing now. I don't know *what* I told her. It just poured out, as if she'd opened a vein. I'm out of practice, socially. I even told her about the kids, about Jenny's partial deafness, about Beth's broken collarbone. I went on for no reason, just to talk into her welcoming face, and instead of following up with the routine questions – for example, "Where do you live, then?" – she simply asked questions such as, "Things are good, between you and your wife?" She spoke like a sideshow medium. She made me even more self-conscious than usual. She made direct personal remarks, which I normally hate. "You missed a spot, here," she said, reaching out and touching my face beneath my jaw.

— She was flirting with you.

— Obviously, but *why*? She picked out the clear loser in the room to flirt with.

— You say that now. You don't look – you never have looked – like a loser, Hart. Try to remember that. Looks count for a great deal.

— Out dribbled my personal life, anyway, except for the things I've been telling you this afternoon. I could hear how pathetic and wet I sounded, but she smiled at me and looked me directly in the eye and did her shrink routine, slicing me up with leading questions. The authorities were building up to the grand prize – people were asked to start the bidding at twenty thousand pounds for a chance to be given a tour of a stately home by the twenty-six-year-old American actress/philanthropist who now owns it – and my new friend—

— Her name?

— Sophie. Sophie realised it was time for us to part. She

pressed her card into my hand and said – I swear, she said this – she said, "I want to know you better, Henry." I didn't even remember having told her my name. "I want to know you better, Henry." Can you believe that?

— Just.

— Now, guess how long it took me to ring Sophie.

— Between four and six weeks.

— Saddler. How did you know? I thought you'd say, sarcastically, "Twelve minutes," or something like that.

— You tried to put her out of your mind for two weeks. For about a further two weeks you thought of nothing else. For about a week after that you gathered up your nerve to dial.

— Spot on. I didn't exactly write out a script for that phone call, but almost. The words "intrigued" and "intimidated" likely figured in what I had to say. She was businesslike and quickly got me to agree to meet her at her flat after work the same day. She said she was a courier for a French television company and very busy. I didn't know what that meant, but it turns out she physically carried documentary footage from one archive to another. I thought these days they just blasted it through the ether, but apparently not always. The first evening she interrogated me some more while she finished dressing and beautifying herself, right in front of me, for her evening on the town. She shared a taxi with me to Marble Arch, kissed me on the lips then skipped away. Thus began my life of adultery, the first step of course being to wash away the scent of Sophie's perfume, which she sprayed into the air and walked through not two feet away from me.

— That would be eau do toilette, not perfume.

— Thanks. I'll try to remember that.

— So, you had a delightful new friend. You spent a guilty week before ringing her again. She said she'd been out of town, and she was so glad to hear from you. She suggested you come right over. You happened to have the late afternoon free. You tore to her flat for half an hour of sex that almost killed you with its intensity, showered on the premises, went to a pub on the way home so that your hair would dry and you would smell naturally of smoke and beer.

— Saddler, you're getting impatient with me. I dare say you've heard this kind of story before. You couldn't have *lived* it.

— I've read a lot, and there's hardly anything else in books. When was the last time you saw her?

— Two weeks ago. Mary doesn't suspect a thing. Everything is going to be fine, and I'll tell you why.

— Are you in love with her?

— With Sophie? Christ, no. Visiting her is like . . . I don't know, it must be the way other chaps feel about going to the gym, not that I've ever done that. She travels a great deal. I saw her on average every ten days or so.

— Past tense?

— Oh, maybe. Who knows? No.

— Do you buy her things?

— Certainly not. It seems a straight-up sexual affair. I feel so adult.

— Hart, you have no idea what you're doing. Your marriage has fallen apart, it's over, and you don't even realise it.

— Rich, coming from you. Don't be silly. I'm just lucky. It settles my mood. I really believe that if Mary ever found out, she would understand. She would approve.

— You're more comprehensively fucked than I thought, Hart.

— Anyway, let me tell you why everything is going to be fine, how I'm going to fix this whole mess. I have only one more thing to tell you—

— Let's see. We've touched on paedophile necrophillia, suspicion of murder, blackmail, an affair. There's more?

— Just a little more, before I limp home to the wife I love.

— Get it over with, then.

— There's more. It happened at work. You know how I used to love my work – and I still do, in theory. You and I first met when we were eight or nine years old. Was I not already interested in maps?

— You were. I remember you had maps on the ceiling of your room.

— Yes. With a torch and binoculars, I used to read and memorise the maps as I lay in bed. The interest in antique maps came much later. As for any collector or dealer, it was the thrill of the chase, the knowing more than the next man. I studied hard.

— I know you did.

— I didn't care if someone had found an antelope skin in a prehistoric cave with a diagram of hunting grounds on it or a copy of a Mercator, I was fascinated. I found them beautiful and inspiring. If you compare maps with books or stamps or coins, I say maps win hands down because of their undeniable usefulness at the time they were made. How many monks' illuminations of the Scriptures does one have to see before getting bored? I know, I know. Some people like that sort of thing, and manuscripts can be beautiful, and it's intriguing to think of how the monks lived. But a map – the science of it, the intuition, the logistics, the execution . . .

— You liked old maps.

— Yes. I had my passion. I thought I could make a living at it – I was sure I could – and this seemed to be confirmed after just a few years. I was young enough not to mind the travel. I met like-minded people. I didn't think many men had it better than I did, making money out of a passion. I knew I was just a middleman, not a collector, not an academic. I knew there were people making a difference in the world – my brother, for example – but I enjoyed my place in the scheme of things and I was certainly doing no harm.

— Speaking of whom, how is the dashing Colin?

— Dashing in both senses. He'll never stop. I can't say I hear too much from him these days. He has every excuse. I think he's in the Congo right now.

— Still with the same outfit?

— Yes. He is full of glory. My point, though, is that I never thought "Oh, I'm peering at this square of paper and wondering how old it is and if it's worth a few thousand quid, when Colin is sewing the arm back on a baby in Liberia. He's fulfilled; the African baby's got its arm. Wonderful. We can't all be Colin. At one extreme you've got the person who blew off the baby's arm, and at the other you've got Colin to sew it back on. The rest of us are middlemen. We sell things. I thought I was lucky to be selling old maps. One of my first trades was a little Pelesquone, of Capri, a thousand years old. I've always loved islands. You get your map, you read up on the cartographer, learn some history. It's all very satisfying. What I do for Rory should be no different. I never wanted to own the maps. I enjoyed having them pass through my hands. I expand my knowledge, even now.

— So your only problem is to earn enough money to pay for school fees and blackmail.

— And until recently the blackmail wasn't such a drain. Do you know what my glottal-stopping blackmailer asked for the first time?

— How much?

— Forty quid.

— You're joking.

— No. He said I was small fry, that he was running a dozen blokes like me, that he wanted to do what was "fair". He seemed to know something about my straitened circumstances.

— Please tell me you didn't pay the man, Hart.

— I did.

— OK, then please tell me that you set a trap for him.

— I didn't. You see, if I'd trapped him, he'd simply set my story loose. I left two twenties in a blank envelope under a builder's skip in Kentish Town.

— My God, Hart, you were enjoying this. You're smiling.

— I know you think I'm a fool, Saddler. I know I *am* a fool. I'm only asking for some empathy on your part. Perhaps, in my shoes, you would never have dug yourself such a deep hole.

— Oh, I'm not so sure.

— Good. I'm telling what happened, as it happened. Let's leave hindsight for later.

— Understood.

— Once a week or so I was asked for forty pounds, and I paid. I never tried to trick the man. He became more talkative. He knew Annette's name, and her parents' names. He knew Cambon's name, too. He knew as much as I did, in other words. One day, about three months into our relationship, he casually said, "You're having nightmares, Mr Hart." Actually, he phrased it as a question, in his fake accent: "You're 'avin' noigh'-mayahs, Mister 'art?" This sent a chill, because I *was* having nightmares. This wasn't unusual for me, especially then, but these were particularly nasty ones. Only Mary knew – in her innocence she suggested I stop drinking wine at dinner. "They've become recurrent," she said. "You curse the fucking this and the fucking that, and you've started shouting, "Not in the foot! Not in the foot!" What is that all about?" Only when she said that did I clearly remember the nightmare. Now I'm no believer in the interpretation of dreams—

— I should hope not. I abhor it, myself.

— Rightly so. But let us give the Viennese shaman the benefit of the doubt for a moment. It relates to my guilt – to my self-perceived guilt – and to a certain instability that may have made me make the misjudgements I'm trying to confess to you now. First of all, I had begun to put myself to sleep at night by recalling my *coup de foudre* in St-Vuis, when I fell in love with Annette before I knew she was a) dead and b) a child. This worked. It warmed me and sent me off to sleep. And then the nightmare followed which, according to Mary, I must have suffered many, many times even before she asked me to sleep in the spare room. I told her I had dreamed that someone was trying to amputate one of my feet. I said I worried I had poor circulation, and that I had lately awakened with numb toes. She thought this sounded reasonable, but of course that wasn't the dream at all. In the dream I was really experiencing, Annette was there, in my hotel room, wearing clothes this time. She also wore the floppy white hat she'd had on in the restaurant with her parents when they thought I was staring at her. She was standing at the foot of the bed. I was lying naked before her, suffering various pains in my body, particularly in my right foot. Annette didn't speak to me, but I understood her thoughts and gestures. She pointed at my right foot and I understood her to be asking me how "it" was "growing". I tried to communicate to her that I had no idea what she meant, but she told me to look at my foot. I did so. My foot was the size of a small dog. In the dream I sat up, horrified. My right foot was not just large, but transparent and throbbing. The centre looked like a sonogram, as if there were a womb in my foot.

— If you say there was a foetus in your foot, Hart, you don't get another drink.

— It wasn't a womb, and it wasn't a foetus. What I had in my distended, pulsating, hideous right foot was a liver.

— A liver? How did you know it was a liver?

— Because in dreams you are "told", or you "know" this sort of information, the same way the girl who isn't speaking asks you if it's "growing", and you know that's what she's asking.

— What's the relevance? You've said you attach no significance to dreams.

— I do think that recurring dreams have significance to the state of mind of the dreamer, especially when he deliberately tries to bring them on by fantasising before sleep.

— So you were revisited by the foot-liver?

— Yes. And other grotesqueries. It was out of Revelation, I tell you. Annette was always there. It became sexual, always with shocking results – just what you'd expect, the whole *vagina dentata* routine, with bells on. You haven't had a nightmare until your penis turns into a cobra that twists around and bites you in the throat.

— I'll admit, I'd be worried. How long did this go on?

— It's still going on.

— Did you follow Mary's advice? No wine before bed? That sounds sensible.

— Certainly I did. And I changed my diet radically in every which direction. I tried going to bed later, going to bed earlier, not to prime the dreams by thinking about that poor girl. But by then she was so lodged in my mind that she made her appearances against my will. I thought about her during the day as well. It nauseated me. I assumed she was a subconscious symbol of my unfathomable guilt.

— But you weren't guilty.

— You keep insisting on that, Saddler. Tell it to the permanent chimerical girl embedded in my psyche. Sure, I could take a step back, tell myself I'd done nothing wrong, show a little backbone, stand up to the hallucinations. It didn't work. To an extent, I gave in. That's what this is all leading up to. I wandered about arguing with myself about morality, about free will, about personal responsibility. It was like the mood that was brought on by seeing you and . . . Sam.

— Why do you hesitate to use his name?

— I've only just learned it. And, to tell you the whole truth, his face has sometimes figured in the nightmares, too. Sorry to involve your lover in my nervous breakdown, Saddler.

— He isn't my lover.

— What is he, then?

— Let's call him my protégé.

— Fine. Your protégé figured in my deteriorating state of mind. Added to that, my blackmailer had upped the ante to one hundred pounds every ten days or so. This was cash I had to find, and to cover up its spending. In this mood, then, I found myself at the home of Mr Ralph Stenniman, who was getting his affairs in order and had a house full of objects he wished to have valued for potential sale. Rory might have taken on this job himself, having seen a portion of Stenniman's stash as it trickled on to the market over the past few years, but Rory was busy with an upcoming auction and he trusted me in the maps department if nowhere else. When I arrived at Stenniman's house, in Surrey, where he had lived for half a century, there were several cars in the drive belonging to other appraisers. It was in no way a grand house, but Stenniman's relentless collecting meant he needed a paintings person, a drawings person, a musical-instruments person, a numismatist, a books person and me, a maps person. We all knew how Stenniman had racked up his treasures. In the early 60s he was a failed orchestral violinist – an accident with his car door – and made a living as a music teacher. He had broad interests, a wife with a bit of money and only one child. It was this child, a boy, who changed everything in Stenniman's life. Stenniman had taught his boy to play the violin and the piano, and the boy's mother, Alicia, had coached the boy's singing voice. They hoped he would become a musician, thinking that was a pleasant way to live at any level of the business. But instead of becoming a classical musician, he joined a pop band. This is before our time, but have you ever heard of someone named Billy Duke?

— No.

— Billy Duke and the Geraniums?

— No.

— Well, neither had I. But for two or three wonderful years Billy Duke – Stenniman's son, real name Peter – stood under a waterfall of money. He was a clever boy. I don't imagine many pop singers saw a lot of return on their work in those days. He was also clever enough to hand over the proceeds to his father for investment. Stenniman was a cultured man, and he invested at first in books and drawings. Like me, he derived pleasure from physically enjoying his investments. Unlike me, he kept everything he bought. Technically the hoard belonged to Peter – to Billy Duke. Unfortunately, the boy could not resist the new temptations of the age and died of a heart attack at the age of twenty-six. Another great surge of record sales followed on the heels of this tragedy, and Stenniman retired to his antiques and his paintings and his maps. At the time I met him he was still only sixty-five years old, but widowed and in poor health. His wife had died long ago. He wanted everything sold before he died – which he hasn't yet done, by the way. Perhaps the influx of raw cash has rejuvenated him. I'm told he has a new girlfriend and for the first time he's found an interest in travel.

— Good for old Stenniman.

— He's a lovely man. He greeted all of us and rushed around trying to be helpful. His collection was not well organised. He had practically no security in the house. He was shy, somewhat stooped, utterly Home Counties, but there was a glint in his eye now that he had decided to part with his things and be liquid at last. He said outright that he feared he had only months to live, and he wanted to know how much money he could give away in his will. He had no relatives. He thought he might set up a local music academy, if we could sell the contents of his house for half a million. There were coughs among the appraisers. I swear, Saddler, a quarter of a million in oils was already staring us in the face before we had our coats off. All morning there were gasps from the experts, upstairs and down. "Thompson, come have a look a this!" from the books man. "Trevor, Jesus!" from the American drawings man. And the oils woman sobbing in the kitchen, having had too much. Most people bring in a crew from one big auction house. Stenniman's idea was to divide and conquer with hungrier, individual appraisers. I'm sure this worked in his favour, even if it took more time. He told me that since the beginning he had bought only objects that "caught his eye", and if so his eye was a marvellous thing and rarely let him down.

— And you dug around in the maps with him?

— Stenniman didn't spend much time with me. He seemed to have shunted his maps to one side over the years. He was not very knowledgeable about them, and hadn't looked them over in two decades. He went from room to room asking the others what was going on, and seemed to be especially proud of his Greek coins. When he wandered over to me I drew his attention to a number of very old Chinese maps – I told him this was not my strongest area, but I could assure him there had to be value there. I whispered that every now and then a "Chinese map" turned out to be something Marco Polo had a hand in. I didn't want to get carried away, or cause the old boy to have a heart attack. Still, he wasn't that interested and he wandered off again. Most of the maps were of the British Isles. Not many real duds among them. There were Roman maps, as well – never my favourites, but there is a market. All I really did on the first day was perform a bit of triage. There was a stack of two dozen maps, including engravings – two copper, one bronze, four silver – that I asked to borrow for deeper analysis. I separated everything into neat piles, wheat from the chaff, and I popped my own pile into my portfolio. I returned ten days later with the good news that Rory's company was prepared to buy half of Stenniman's map collection for just under two hundred thousand pounds, and auction the remainder in six months' time at a fifteen-per-cent commission. Then I returned the maps to him . . .

— Yes?

— I returned the maps to him . . . All except one.

— Oh, Hart, you *didn't*.

— . . .

— Tell me you didn't, Hart.

— I did. I'd like to say I fell in love with a particular object, that I wasn't in a straight frame of mind, that I kept it because it magically stuck to my fingers and I couldn't shake it free. I'd *like* to say all of that, and the state-of-mind bit would be partially true. But enough time has gone by. I am a thief.

— What did you take?

— A silver engraving, roughly twelve by nine inches, four millimetre thick, tarnished to black – in the pile at Stenniman's house it had looked like a piece of burned parchment. It hadn't been in the same stack as the other metals. It was tucked behind the back leaf of a six-hundred-year-old atlas. When I got back to Rory's shop I put it aside for myself, as if I already knew it was something I'd want to hold on to. I farmed out the maps I needed experts to look at, I filed the maps I could value myself, and I took the silver tablet home. I cleaned it in the kitchen, as one would a pair of candlesticks.

— Just tell me what it was, Hart.

— Well, obviously, it was an engraved map. A positive, therefore not for printing. Now, a cartographer isn't going to be an engraver, usually – who has the time? So your engravings are by definition copies. And old maps, let's face it, are cut-and-paste jobs. The master cartographer sits at the centre of a web. He'll snatch a morsel here, a titbit there, get the latest word from an explorer of the high seas, glom it all together into an approximate whole and call it a representation of his surrounding world. What features does he wish to include? Well, as I've been telling you, all of history is there in the priorities of the cartographer: your caveman draws a picture of a hunting trail, embellished perhaps by a stream crossing or a pond; your Egyptian says, "Walk three hours in the direction of the sunrise and you'll reach the river"; your ultra-clever Greek just wants to show off his maths and geometry; your dogged Roman wants to chart his impressive roads and sites of conquest; your Dark Ages cartographer knows he should just shut up, live a quiet life; your Italian mariner wants to get from A to B on the Med without hugging the headlands. What I had here, with this silver sheet, was not made for printing – you wouldn't use silver, anyway – it was a representation, gorgeous, a work of art to set the master cartographer's vision in stone, as it were. It had no practical use, though. It's probably better to call it jewellery than a map. You wouldn't take it on the road. I decided right away that the engraving dated back to the twelfth century.

— How did you know?

— Because it's dated in the cartouche. Also, the lie of the land.

— Which was?

— France and Spain.

— Is that important?

— Let me just tell you how this map was executed. I wish I had it here to show you, but we'd need lights and a magnifying glass. The only analogy I can make is to microchips. Do you know how microchips are made?

— Not the faintest.

— Let's just say they're not made with tiny Chinese fingers. They're printed. But this silver plate had been worked on by someone wielding – God, I still don't know – some sort of tool so inconceivably sharp and tiny and *hard*. Whoever did this could write out your name in a full stop.

— Angels on the head of a pin?

— Without getting mystical, Saddler, this chap could engrave all the streets of modern London – the Knowledge, say – on the palm of your hand. And write the street names. I've been over this thing with a microscope. I need 120-X power to read some of the lettering. A speck of dust could blot out a word.

— Come on.

— There's never been anything like it. I have no idea how it was done. Today you'd do it on silicon. You'd get the molecules to move electronically.

— Is that what you're saying happened? Hundreds of years ago?

— Not at all. Not in silver. And they had no electricity.

— That we know of.

— You're way ahead of me, Saddler.

— I know where you're going with this, Hart. Aliens. Aliens

made your map. Are you sure you've had enough to drink this afternoon? Now, about these aliens.

— These aliens would have to be Christian aliens to have wanted to engrave this particular map. It's a map of that old Catholic pilgrim route. The Compostela. If I dared show it to anyone yet, I'd put money on some sort of hitherto unknown technology, for its period. Do you think it's possible to use – I don't know, *sunlight* to make such an engraving?

— I'm no scientist.

— To me, this map just reeks of high tech. At first I imagined the drawing being etched into glass, somehow, at twenty times the size, and then blasting focused sunbeams through the glass onto the silver plate. But the more one studies ancient art, the more one just has to admit that they were bloody good at what they did: they took their time, they were perfectionists. I think it's just possible that an engraver somewhere sat down for about fifteen years making this map using a micro-stylus with a diamond tip. Talk about a steady hand.

— Any idea who made the map, rather than the engraving itself?

— I've narrowed it down to three men, all of whom worked in southern France in the twelfth century. I'm going to need expert help, but of course I can't show them the engraving without telling them where I found it.

— Or making up an elaborate lie.

— Which I've already planned to do. I'd thought of saying it was found in my wife's late father's possessions.

— But Mary's father died – what, five years ago?

— Six. That's even better, you see. The engraving sat in storage for all these years. We decided to clean out his belongings once Mary had got through a long period of mourning. That sort of thing. This way it belongs to me, at least vicariously. And at least long enough to get a friendly expert to tell me what it is. That is what I'd *planned* to do. But I changed my mind. I've decided to tell whoever needs to know that it belongs to Darius Saddler.

— To me? Hart, I'm shocked enough as it is. What are you thinking?

— You found it among your late parents' things. It's the same lie as I was going to tell about Mary, only you won't *mind*.

— I mind already, Hart. Jesus.

— Ah, but you'll go along with this.

— Why would I do that?

— Because you owe me.

— I *owe* you? Please explain why that is so, Hart.

— It's late. Another time.

## London, 19 September

Henry Hart and Darius Saddler meet, one week after their previous conversation, in the basement bar of the restaurant Yours, off Kensington High Street. Hart's dark hair is still wet from showering. He wears the same suit as last time. He still appears tense, and his pale face is drawn. Saddler wears a pristine white linen suit. Once again Saddler appears far more relaxed than his friend; he leans back in his chair and crosses his long legs.

—I'd be very interested to know how you remember it, Saddler. We've never talked about those times in all these years. I've thought about them, though.

— I don't know which times you're referring to.

— I'll just tell you what I recall, from my point of view. Feel free to correct my interpretation.

— I will.

— We were eighteen years old. We had it all figured out. We'd read our Nietschze. We were a secret society of two, right?

— That's how I remember it, yes. We passed in wider society as conformists. Privately we marked out a superior trajectory through life. We were a couple of loathsome little Nazis.

— And our first step?

— To take a pass on university. We were already overeducated, in our own opinion.

— University was for sheep. University was for "careers". "Career" was a dirty word. We were too clever for that, weren't we, Saddler? We knew everything already. We were nihilists.

— Insofar as the word "nihilist" had anything to do with the friend's unoccupied bedsit where we hatched our plans.

— That was one of the terms we used. Lying to blameless, unsuspecting parents – telling them that our permanent abandonment of the conventional life was a "gap year" – that was our first act. Shunning our drug-addled, feckless, shallow contemporaries . . .

— Which one of us do you think was responsible, Hart?

— To outsiders, I'll bet they thought it was you. I was the dark horse. I was more reserved, immature and uncertain. Our grand scheme could only have been set in train by you – the more worldly, intellectual, outgoing, rumoured-to-be-Jewish Darius Saddler. You were considered audacious. Besides, you were better-looking. But no. It was I, the retiring, bookish Henry Hart, swallowing a teenaged epiphany whole, who had been the first to argue that it was possible to outwit the Machine.

— We really called it that?

— I remember this vividly. One had to treat the Machine as if it were a superior officer, or a prefect, or a wicked stepmother. This required cunning, disguise, misdirection, stealth, patience, fearlessness and consistency. We made a pact, in writing, which we signed and vowed to uphold—

— And then we burned the document over a gas cooker. The flames briefly illuminated the solemn faces of a pair of idiotic teenagers who at that moment thought they were the only ones in the world with the insight, spirit and courage to conquer the Machine. What a couple of twits.

— Oh, I don't know about that, Saddler. I think we were relatively grown up. We'd already been friends for ten years, but we weren't like "brothers": we weren't like those backslapping sportsmen, not like the other boys whose families went on holiday together, certainly not like the gangs of hyper-socialising girls. No, we had a more private and considerably faster bond. That's how I remember it.

— I agree. I still think it's amusing. Remember how we were always supposedly "five moves ahead"? We thought we were prepared for all the traps – social, academic, romantic. We were perpetually in a position to outmanoeuvre the Machine.

— There was no friction between us. Only the rare misunderstanding.

— We were close friends, Hart.

— We weren't equals, though. I looked up to you. Especially when you began to speak mysteriously of "an older woman at City College". You were so casual about her, and her "suicide attempts". You were doing that to make me feel immature and inexperienced – which of course I was.

— You always had a girlfriend.

— Always? Oh, sure, for approximately six months in our final year, a girl who refused to have intercourse with me. But not a glamorously suicidal older woman from City College. You never told me her name. You hinted that she was *foreign*.

— You soon realised why I had to . . . why I had to embellish the facts.

— Why you had to lie. And I didn't realise soon enough, Saddler. I thought all the secrecy had to do with your older woman being engaged to someone else. I thought you were living by our creed. When you occasionally disappeared for a couple of days and returned looking sallow, shagged out, thoroughly *crumpled* by your adventures, I suppose it only stirred me to greater philosophical pronouncements on the Edge and the Wilderness. What a sad, credulous child I was.

— I don't remember you that way, Hart. You were a leader of men. I was fully prepared to follow you into the unknown.

— And then your grandfather died.

— My step-grandfather.

— Yes, but I didn't know that at the time. I knew next to

nothing about your family. I was touched when you invited me to the memorial. I'd tried so hard to build up the old nihilist shell, and I wanted to believe that any nihilist worth his view of the empty, pitiless universe ought to be able to ignore anyone's death – the death of his own child, if it came to that – particularly that of a quiet old man who had lived his life very much inside the circuitry of the Machine. Sure, you posed as best you could after hearing the news. Your nonchalance lasted about a quarter of an hour, as you pretended not to give a damn. Then you collapsed into tears, said you'd loved your grandfather –

— Step-grandfather.

— and you needed me to hold your hand at the memorial. You said, "Perhaps it's time you met the family." I remember I said, "I'll forgive you this one lapse," probably dabbing at a tear or two of my own. My nihilist armour had been pierced. Besides, I was curious about your family. I think it's interesting that in all of those years I'd never met a single one of them. I'd waved at them out of car windows, and you had read to me from their letters. I had the impression that these people were modern, liberal-minded, well-off. I knew you called your *step*-grandfather by his first name—

— Nathan.

— Nathan. And that he was American, therefore an oddity. The way you told the story, he'd done something monstrous.

— Did I put it that way? I was trying to make him more interesting than he probably was.

— He came to London during the war – "something to do with refugees", you said. He'd stayed on and never set foot in his homeland again. In doing so he left behind an ex-wife, a three-year-old daughter and a formerly close American family who would never speak to him again. He married an English war widow who had an eight-year-old son.

— That would be my father.

— Old Nathan had been widowed ten years previously, and

for that time he had lived with you and your parents and sisters. What I wanted to know was what happened to all of those Jews back in America. Had they really never communicated with Nathan ever again?

— You soon found out. Believe me, I was as surprised as you were.

— Come on, Saddler. You were withholding information, as usual. You have to think of it from my point of view. I showed up at the memorial, thinking the old Richmond mansion was *your house*.

— It belonged to a friend. We wanted to use his garden.

— Your harried mother took me by the elbow and got the introductions started. I assumed that the Saddler family always operated at frenetic pitch, but I gradually began to realise that hardly anyone knew each other and the Americans had crashed the memorial en masse.

— Hah. You're talking about a day that has entered family lore. I first learned about all of the unexpected arrivals just the night before, as did my poor parents. Nathan's ex-wife and daughter, Nathan's younger brother and his younger sister and their spouses and children, on and on. And, at the last minute—

— Nathan's actual *mother*.

— Incredible. We were outnumbered two to one. And the strong family resemblance to Nathan, it was so pronounced, it looked as if the English people had wandered in on a Jewish ceremony back home in New Jersey. That was enough to stir the pot, but in addition many relatives of Nathan's widow's war-dead first husband – technically my family – had taken it upon themselves to attend, in large numbers. It seemed to my camp that there might be a secret will to contest.

— I remember what you said: "A man quietly imports fruit, and look at the chaos he causes." You were very suave. In my eyes you grew into an adult during the course of one afternoon. You were graceful. Everyone was knocked out by your speech.

— My non-speech. It was my sister's idea that we play charades. I was pretty choked up, in any case.

— I thought the audience would never get your clues. "Sieve" was hard. "Ill" had you pretending to vomit. Anyway, I wasn't the only one who was moved when the crowd shouted "Civilised!" in unison. Well done, Saddler. You had set the tone. From then on, in honour of the memory of a civilised man, the three families mingled for the rest of the afternoon and found much to discuss. I was free to flirt with your sister, who had recently turned sixteen.

— I remember seeing that. What *was* Lily saying to you?

— The first thing she said to me was, "You're taller than I thought you'd be. I was expecting a smaller person." And I said, "Is that so? Your brother described me?" "No, no," said your little sister, "I imagined you on my own." Naturally she arched her back and batted her lashes at me. I thought those huge eyes of hers were begging me to take her somewhere and kiss her. That is what I believed. I said, "I'm surprised Darius ever mentioned me." "Oh, he did, that's for sure." I honestly thought I was playing along with an over-sophisticated girl's come-on. I said, "Darius told me about you, too. He told me how pretty and grown-up you were." It was you, Saddler, who had trained me to use direct flattery with girls. You were the charmer. I smiled at your sister and said, "How right he was." Don't laugh, Saddler. She said, "I don't know why, but I expected someone . . . I don't know, blond?" I said, "I've disappointed you." "Oh, not at *all*," Lily said. She reached out and touched my sleeve. Jesus. "It's better that you're the way you are."

— Good old Lily.

— It gets worse. She asked me, "Why do you think Darius waited until now to introduce you to all of us?" I was so clueless. I said, "I don't know, what do you mean?" "You've been friends for ten years. I've been hearing about you since I was a tiny girl." I explained to Lily that although it might seem strange, we were never that sort of friends. And she said, "I understand. And my parents do, too." All this time I was still wondering where I could take Lily to kiss her, assuming that would be all right with you. Then she asked me if I had introduced you to my family, and when I said I hadn't she said, "You probably ought to reciprocate. Or perhaps your parents aren't ready?" I swear, Saddler, I thought you'd betrayed our plans not to go to university. I thought that's what Lily had been talking about. I said, "I'm sure they're ready. And your parents – they're *au courant*?" She didn't know the expression. She wrinkled her nose. "They know what's going on?" And Lily said, "Oh, completely. And don't you worry. I just know they'll approve. They're almost embarrassing, they're so open-minded."

— She was a wicked tease.

— Well, *I* didn't know that. I said to her, "I'll be staying at your parents' house. And you?" "I'll be there." So I smiled at her and said that, for the time being, we had to tear ourselves away from each other and circulate with the guests. She said, "Avoid the Americans." By that I thought she meant the Jews, as it seemed you'd told her so much about me.

— What?

— About my anti-Semitism.

— You were anti-Semitic?

— No, no. You remember that essay of mine that caused a problem.

— Oh, right. "Where Hitler and I Part Company". I thought people got the joke.

— They really didn't, Saddler. So I thought she a) wanted to meet me secretly at your parents' house later on, and b) that I was a crazy anti-Semite she'd thought would be "blond". And I thought, so this is Saddler's world. What could you and I have talked about, for ten years, without even superficial information having been exchanged? How incurious I must have been, and how unforthcoming about my own home life. For ten years, you had gone home not only to parents and sisters, but to the civilised foreign widower who, blood relation or not, must have helped to form your character. A family with secrets was fascinating to me. A grandfather living at least a triple life was glamorous. I imagined that there was even more to Nathan's story. "Something to do with refugees?" An American who never went home after the war? The importation of fruit? To me it all reeked of espionage – for CIA and Mossad, both. I decided I would grill you – or, more likely, Lily – the moment I had a chance. My own life was an open book by comparison, and so conventional there was probably an acronym to categorise it in its totality. I'd never had to spell it out, but what could be more *normal* than the son of a GP father and a Tory-activist mother? The younger brother of a too-handsome and too-promising medical student? You seemed to have the goods here – Jewish-American spy mentor, radical-seeming parents with money, one sexy, upfront sister and another getting that way, an older woman at City College and secrets in every corner of that crowded garden.

— All of this seems really to have stuck in your mind.

— Oh, yes. You on your haunches talking to your previously unknown nineteenth-century step-great-grandmother, hoping she understood that charades had been played because you had been too clogged with emotion to speak. You patted her knee as you stood up. As you did so you caught my eye across the garden and hurried over. You told me to be so kind as to mingle with some of your relatives. "The East End ones," you said. And so I mingled with the East Enders, who only sounded that way but were really from Putney. Two hours later we were back at your parents' house, and the scale of your crimes began to come into focus.

— Please, Hart.

— You shamelessly took advantage of me. Before I'd even had a chance to pursue your sister, thinking I'd done my job at the memorial and you were finished with my services for the day, I found myself having an uncomfortable tête-à-tête with your father in his study. Uncomfortable because at first I didn't have the faintest idea what he was talking about. He was exhausted, having buried his stepfather and coped with the relatives, and maybe he was slightly drunk. Strange to think that he was only a few years older than we are now. He was greying and had that deep voice I suppose you have inherited. He told me to call him "Roger", after I'd tried "Professor Saddler". He told me to serve myself from a grown-up tray of brandies. We settled into armchairs like a pair of old gents at their club. It was too warm for a fire, so there was nothing for me to look at but your father. Why are you laughing?

— I like the way you're trying to set the scene.

— Don't be condescending. So I sat there with your father, eyes tearing in cognac fumes, and wondered where the hell you were hiding – you, your mother and sisters. It wasn't a big house. Where had you all gone? To bed? Why was it so quiet? Anyway, I thought I knew why I was there. Lily had already told me – so I believed. Your father was about to grill me about our decision not to go to university, ever. He would say he didn't blame me, though he suspected it was my idea; he would say he'd had the same instincts when he was my age; he would say by all means enjoy a gap year if we could find the money, and then he would urge me in the strongest terms to reconsider. I could hear his words already: "Take it from me: you can't see what I know from your side of experience, but this would be the biggest mistake you will ever make in your life." His argument would carry extra weight because he was modern, he was relaxed, he wanted me to call him "Roger", he taught Marxist theory, he probably hated the Machine as much as I did. I was prepared for the lecture and determined to be polite in my defiance. Roger cleared his throat, looked at me and said what a pleasure it was to meet me at last. He thanked me for coming to the memorial, and he apologised for all the confusion. I noticed that he couldn't maintain eye contact and kept looking down into his glass, which needed almost immediately to be refilled. It was when he did get a refill, then sat down again looking at a loss for words, that I realised he was nervous.

— My old dad, nervous?

— Don't play the innocent. You had set this up. In retrospect I feel sorry for your father. After telling me what a pleasure, and so on, he tried to get to the point. That's when we began to speak at cross purposes, or right past each other. "I wanted you to know, Henry, that I . . . That is, that my wife and I . . . That we . . . That we love Darius very much and are one hundred per cent supportive." This surprised me. I'd thought he was going to lay down the law. So I said so: "God, Roger, what a relief. I was sure you would disapprove. More than that, I thought you'd put a stop to it." "Disapprove? Put a stop? How could we disapprove? How could we put a stop?" He went on to say how pleased he was that everything was out in the open. That he thought the situation "mature". He thought the time was right, he said it could never have happened in his day, and that he hoped everything would work out for the best. I grinned away and agreed with everything he said. Then he asked me, "Do your parents know?" I said, "No, not yet." Did I expect that to be difficult? Yes. When did I plan on telling them? I'd put it off as long as I could, though I didn't like to deceive them. I said they were not so open-minded as he and his wife seemed to be. Roger said he understood completely, that I'd have to negotiate my "relationship" with my parents as I saw fit. My relationship with my parents? I assured him my relationship was perfectly good. "I'm sure it is," said your father, drinking deeply and trying to smile.

— This could have gone on indefinitely.

— No doubt. But at that point your mother came into the study. She'd probably been in the kitchen, staring at the clock, giving your father and me half an hour to sort things out man to man. She'd changed from mourning-black dress to left-wing-environmentalist uniform. Not that there was anything wrong with your father, but seeing your mother was a relief – so fresh and vital. A font of carefree energy. She sat down on the padded fender, patted my knee and said, "You've had your little *talk*, I hope?" I said that we had, and that I was grateful for Roger's support. I noticed that her throat was red, as if someone had been trying to strangle her. She was forcing her cheerfulness. She *exhaled* each word as she said, "I'm *so* glad this is *out* in the *open*. *Gosh*." As the blood rose in her cheeks, it drained from mine. Your father had kept a poker face. Your mother expressed the whole truth with that one word, "*Gosh*." She was straining every liberal tendon in her body to appear to welcome into her home her son's homosexual lover.

— You could see that?

— *No*, I couldn't see that. Jesus Christ, Saddler. I'm telling you this in retrospect. I spent the next three days in the bosom of your family, utterly ignorant or subconsciously in denial of what was going on around me. I thought we'd cleared the air about university plans, that's all, while everyone else was in a state of shock and thinking I was your boyfriend. Three days I lounged around the place, getting comfortable. In my own little head I was looking for ways to get your sister alone, while the rest of you were talking about "sleeping arrangements" and putting you and me together in the downstairs bedroom so we wouldn't be inhibited in our bloody all-night lovemaking. *Jesus*.

— When did the penny drop?

— The penny didn't drop – Lily threw it at me. I finally got my hands on her during a walk, professed my love and so on, and she accused me of "cheating" on you. The truth swirled grotesquely into view. She told me the whole story. You'd come out to your parents only two weeks before, when Nathan died, and it must have seemed a good idea to get a lot of emotions on the table at the same time. She said she'd "known all along". You'd invited me to stay so that your parents would see that you had a steady, respectable boyfriend. God, I still gnash my teeth.

— But, as I recall, you went along with it.

— Indeed I did. Only Lily knew that I was pretending. Didn't you notice a little campness in my bearing, a pursing of the lips?

— I can't say that I did.

— Well, perhaps I'm no good at camp. But I thought I was dropping the right cultural references. Schubert, that sort of thing.

— Schubert? *Schubert?*

— Wasn't he . . . ?'

— No.

— Anyway, Lily promised that if I went along with the ruse, she'd let me fondle her naked body.

— *Really*. And?

— I fondled her naked body. I don't want to talk about that. It is a sacred minute of my life. I just wanted you to know that even fondling Lily was not repayment enough for what I went through on your behalf. That, Saddler, is only the first of the reasons why you owe me.

— I don't get it.

— Not yet you don't. It wasn't simply that I found myself having to pose as your gay lover – which I can't say I was doing, I was just playing along. It's that I'd had no idea you were gay in the first place. You won't believe me, but I had only the vaguest idea that such a condition existed in the real world. I thought men-with-men was something twisted in books, or something Shakespeare was falsely accused of, something ballet dancers pretended to be. I thought it was a grand aesthetic, a posturing, an approach to life. I didn't know it was something people really were, or did.

— Hart, you have *got* to be kidding.

— Not at all. Why do you think I've never brought this up in twenty years? We could have had a laugh about the whole episode, if I'd really had a clue what was going on. And because I didn't, and because it took me about five more years to accept that your . . . your *inclination* wasn't just a sophisticated affectation, I didn't want to admit how stupid and naïve and *inferior* I was. I didn't want you to think I was that innocent. I promise you, I had absolutely no idea. I admit, I'm still coming to grips with the concept.

— If that's the case, then you were playing a lot of games.

— I . . . What?

— . . .

— Don't look at me that way, Saddler. What are you talking about, "games"?

— If you don't know, it's not worth getting into now.

— Wait a minute. Do you mean . . . ? You thought I was . . . ?

— It would have been convenient.

— Oh, Saddler, for Christ's sake. *Me?*

— I suppose I learned that wishing doesn't make things so. Anyway I can see you're horrified. Feel free to change the subject.

— Horrified isn't what I am. Sorry to appear that way. Taken aback, maybe. Are you telling me that when you introduced me to your parents, came out and all that, you believed we were . . . I don't know the word.

— Courting?

— Oh, *fuck*.

— I was as young as you were, remember. I don't know what I *could* have been thinking.

— For one thing you'd been lying to me about the older woman at City College. That *was* a lie, right?

— It was an older *man* at City College.

— All right, I'll just put to you the question I've been dying to ask since those days. I'm going to ask if you've ever slept with a woman.

— Slept with, yes. If you mean sex, not in any form you would recognise by the name. I was platonically in love with Caroline Sescher for about three years, before she died.

— Saddler, she was about eighty years old.

— Couldn't help it. Loved her to death, so to speak. Now can we get back to your bloody map? You're making me nervous. You say I "owe" you. Maybe I did embarrass you, but I don't think any lasting harm was done.

— That's where you're oh, so very wrong. And *you're* the one who was playing games. That little fondle I got from your sister Lily? You know perfectly well what that fondle . . . enlarged into. I don't know how you found out – I'm guessing Lily told you. But Lily was my first. I was Lily's first. And it lasted for nine months. Admit to me that you knew this.

— I did.

— I was . . . I don't want to break down here, you *bastard*, but . . . In retrospect, Lily was the . . . Lily was the love of my life. I still think about her every hour, to this day. The breathlessness of the whole thing, the having to sneak about, the illegality. It's like you and that *boy*.

— Sam.

— Sure, "Sam".

— And where did you and Lily go?

— You know damned well where we went. You were probably following us.

— I never followed you.

— We did what young people did twenty years ago. Dancing, finding a place to be alone together. But you destroyed the affair. What did you tell her, Saddler? That I was gay? That I had a disease? You sabotaged the whole thing, I know you did. Did you simply tell your parents? Is that what you did? Did you get your parents to put a stop to it? Because after those months there was not even a cooling-off, not a reconsideration on Lily's part. There was a nothing, a rupture, a silence. Let's get this over with and have you confess.

— I . . . I confess. I told my parents. Christ, Hart, she was sixteen years old.

— Rich, coming from you.

— At the time . . .

— I'm explaining why you *owe* me.

— I understand. I'm truly sorry. Who knows how it might have worked out? I can't apologise enough. I admit that I owe you. Tell me how you expect me to palm off the map as my parents'.

— OK. Apology sort of accepted, even though forgiveness is beyond me until you do as I ask. There's money in it. I get the feeling you wouldn't say no to a windfall right now. Fix up your stables, flog the chateau?

— I don't think you've thought this through. You've already stolen the map, correct? If it's all that valuable, people are going to want to know where it comes from. You'll say it came from the effects of my late parents. They never owned anything remotely like that. And what would I tell my sisters?

— You lie to them too, obviously. Or pay them to keep quiet. I don't know.

— You are *so* desperate.

— How is Lily, anyway? Is divorce agreeing with her?

— No. She's quite sad and scared. She's had a rotten time. A rotten life, really. Maybe you shouldn't have fondled her and *enlarged* the situation. Who's going to buy your bloody map, and for how much?

— Let me tell you something about collectors. I mean the truly hard-core, obsessive, lifelong addict collectors. I don't care what it is – motor cars, stamps, glass figurines – name it, they're so bloody monomaniacal, they eat and sleep their *craving*. It's pathological. I've hung out with these crazies. They'd quite literally kill for the last piece of whatever puzzle it is they think they're putting together. I'd wager map people are pretty much the worst of the lot. It's like anything: the majority are in it as a relaxing hobby – the way I might have been if I hadn't made maps my livelihood – but at the fringes they're like junkies or . . . well, like paedophiles, since we were on the topic. They'll never be satisfied. They obsess so deeply, it's hard to imagine how they look out of their eyes at the world. All they see is the object of their desires. If something like my silver map comes to them out of nowhere, they'll be *frothing* for it.

— How much?

— Hang on, I'm explaining. You find three or four of these psychos – I know the ones I'd approach – and play them off each other. That would be good enough, but I have an ace in the hole.

— Which is?

— The fucking Vatican.

— I'm fascinated.

— It's the same sort of leverage I tried to bring in on deals in the old days – the Taiwan, the Hawaii and so on. Bring in a government to up the stakes – or at least mention a government's potential interest. The Vatican buys an unreal amount of art – and relics and books and just plain old documentation. They buy into their own history. Some of this they acquire in order to hide it. Do you know how much pornography the Vatican is sitting on? There is Catholic significance to my map. The Vatican may have an interest either in publicising the Compostela route, or in suppressing it. They might arrange kickbacks from the towns mentioned as Compostela pilgrim sites that aren't used today – one of which, coincidentally, is what today we call St-Vuis. I don't care. And in any case the map has intrinsic value as a work of art and jewellery.

— You know someone at the Vatican?

— I can get to a German cardinal, through old Andreas.

— Will you tell Andreas about the map?

— I hardly think that's necessary. And the Church won't tell him, either. What I'm vaguely hoping is that the Vatican will understand, *sub rosa*, that the map's provenance is iffy, and that they might agree to pay me to keep it under wraps for a long period of time. Like until I'm dead. They justifiably have a long view. I'm assuming the Vatican is gangrenously corrupt.

— Probably a safe bet. Now, how much? How much will your crime pay?

— Crime? Hah. I'm returning to the pact. *Our* pact, Saddler, if you remember. I'm not taking it lying down any longer. I'm sick of the bad guys winning.

— You want to be a bad guy?

— In my small way, yes. I'm not saying this is a victimless crime, but nearly. Maybe a clarinet player won't have a practice room. Stenniman got this map how? A dead pop-star son who made hundreds of thousands on the back of a song called 'You Can Whoo Whoo'. And accidentally – accidentally – one of the old man's books had a map stuck inside it that no one would have found for all time if it hadn't been for me, nor recognised what it was if it hadn't been for me. So, number one, I'm taking something that philosophically speaking doesn't necessarily *exist*. And, number two, in exchange for my services to Stenniman and the map world in general I am taking a one-hundred-per-cent cut of the proceeds.

— Who are the bad guys you're joining?

— Worse guys. Tax cheats, fat cats, bullies, liars. Intimidators, frauds, bribers, dictators, aggressors, strongmen, pimps. Anyone who cheats and subjugates and has his way regardless. The tramplers. Drug dealers, bookies, purveyors of child pornography. Those who take advantage. Pharmaceuticals. Italians. Bent coppers. The prick who's blackmailing me. I can't baulk now at an invisible crime – the beneficiaries being my wife and daughters, immediately and directly – when any visit to a City pub urinal has one pissing next-porcelain to people who do this day in and day out and for what reward? *Everything*. Their reward is temporal happiness and security. Fuck 'em. I want in.

— I love to see you so fired up. I'll ask again: how much?

— First, let's look at the downside.

— Getting caught.

— That's it. Getting caught. I believe there is a one-in-a-thousand chance. Because I'll only be selling to secretive types who're up to their stinking armpits in unscrupulousness already, they're not going to blab. The money would go to Switzerland, like all the bad guys' money. I already have an account. Well, not in Switzerland, they wouldn't have me. Liechtenstein, a decade ago. Same thing, almost. Just to make you feel comfortable with the idea, here's the worst case. I sell my map to someone – a Dutch tax exile in Monaco, for example. For some unlikely reason he's dissatisfied and tries to sell it on. The next person in line wants provenance. My name comes up. I point to you. You crack under Interpol torture and spill the beans. Stenniman is revealed as the rightful owner – if he's still alive. I am exposed as a thief. You are fingered as my passive accomplice.

— This is supposed to make me feel comfortable?

— What's the worst they could do to us? Your basic fat cat does this all the time – and far worse – and you never see them doing bird, do you? Not unless they physically killed someone with their own hands, and even then . . .

— "Doing bird?" You're out of control.

— Remember, Saddler, this crime's a fait accompli. It's not as if we're sitting here hatching a plot to steal the Crown Jewels. The heist is behind us. I have already, figuratively, abseiled into the viewing room, evaded the laser beams and tiptoed along the cable-stays of Tower Bridge with the Jubilee Crown, or whatever it is, cupped in my hands. All right? The trail is cold, and no one's following it anyway. Trust me, it's foolproof.

— How *much*?

— I'd be disappointed with less than a million and a half, sterling.

— Oh, *Christ*.

— You like? I would happily offer you right now ten per cent against the extremely unlikely eventuality that I'm forced to tell someone where I found the map, and against the even unlikelier eventuality that you would not be believed when you ever-so-insouciantly claim the map had belonged to your late parents, via your late step-grandfather, the mysterious American Jew who had "something to do with refugees" during the Second World War. Do you see how it's falling into place?

— Well. Perhaps you have thought this through. And it's true that I need the money. God *knows*, I need the money. I'm financially exposed. In fact, financially, I'm running naked and on fire around Trafalgar Square.

— Really?

— Just last week, while you were with your friendly accountant, I had the most extraordinary conversation on the phone with my plumber, Patrice, down in France. I'd explained that it was likely I would be renting out the west wing of the house as early as a year from now if all other work goes well. The plumber, making notes, mentioned that I'm going to need special, ultra-strong pipes and rivets and bolts for the main shower-room sink. "All hotels know this," he said. "You think, for yourself, it's just the one time you fuck on the sink. In the hotels it's every day. Some of these ladies, they're not so trim as yourself. Big, fat German women are going to get fucked every day, maybe twice a day, on your sink. You're talking about eighty kilos of woman being pumped up and down on your sink for maybe an hour every day, and that's not just her, that's her fat Boche friends, too. Your *locataires* won't just be sitting on the sink. And they won't be little. The man will haul his fat wife up onto the thing and start fucking her while singing 'Die Wacht am Rhein' at the top of his lungs, banging, banging, banging. You get that rhythm going, the big fat woman bouncing her hippo arse, your sink won't last the first morning. Like I said, everyone in the hotel business knows this. The sink in the shower room has got to be plumbed like a fucking bank vault." Patrice wants to charge me twenty-three thousand euros.

— You see?

— I have to think here.

— Shake on it?

— I'm thinking, I'm thinking. You've given me so much

information. You have a lot more to sort out in your life than just the map.

— The pact, Saddler. *Our* pact. Come on, shake.

— Oh . . . Here, then.

— Thanks, Saddler. You won't regret it.

— One more thing I have to ask, before we go our separate ways. I really do wonder. Mostly when I talk to someone who has children, they won't shut up about them. You've hardly mentioned your girls. I find that odd.

— Hold on a sec while I *shudder* with relief.

— Relief?

— That I never had a son, Saddler.

— Why is that?

— Because my girls will *never* be ashamed of me.

## London, 16 October

It has been a month since Hart and Saddler last spoke. This time they meet for late lunch at a Thai restaurant in the West End. Hart is making every effort to appear more relaxed than he has in the past. He wears casual clothing. Saddler has lost his tan and wears a fresh-from-the-cemetery black suit and tie.

—You're looking well, Saddler.

— Hah.

— Is it the prospect of all that loot?

— On the contrary. I'm a nervous wreck. I've wanted to ring you every day, but I was afraid you'd think I was a coward.

— It's a good thing you didn't. We shouldn't be using the telephone except to arrange to go out for a drink or dinner, like this. No mail, electronic or otherwise. There's nothing we have to discuss at this point, anyway. I only want to keep you informed.

— I can tell you're enjoying the skulduggery. Meeting only in public. No phone. Need-to-know.

— I must admit, having a project like this has put a spring in my step. It's true that I was getting a little down for a while there. As you must have noticed. That old adolescent alienation was reborn. I was beginning to remember what alienation really means, and feels like. Alienated from society, from other people, from the whole culture. You could see how I was, Saddler. Unfocused. Looking for problems where none existed. Blaming myself.

Bitching about fat cats when all I did was envy them. I felt I was just oozing along, waiting to die. That's the way I consciously thought: "I'm waiting to die." There was no joy in anything, anymore, if there ever had been. You'll say it's self-pity –

— I haven't said it yet, though.

— – and maybe that's true, but taking this first step, I tell you, it's a remarkable feeling. I feel better walking down the street, I notice things that give me pleasure. I sometimes feel a fondness for London again, if I ever did in the first place. I show up at Rory Fine's shop and we exchange confident *banter*, instead of my staring at my shoes and waiting for orders from the big man. It's as if I'd regained a sense of taste I hadn't known I'd lost, and had tucked into a . . . I don't know . . .

— Fried Camembert?

— If you like. And here's an interesting thing: Mary.

— You've told her everything, of course.

— No, Saddler, and don't be sarcastic. But it's as if I didn't have to tell her. It's affected her by osmosis. As I told you before – I didn't want to dwell on it – Mary was in a bad way. Far too thin, grey-looking, seeming to be under a dark cloud all the time, lashing out at me and the girls. She was losing her hair, too, actually. When I went home after last time, a little the worse for wear, obviously, she demanded to know what I'd "told" you about our "problems". Mary is obsessed with appearances. When I said you and I had only talked about old times, we'd just reminisced, she turned stone cold and didn't speak to me for days. I think she's jealous of you. I never sit around drinking and reminiscing with *her*, you see. With us it always has to be about the children. Gradually, though, and being as pleasant as I could be, she turned around. She always does in the end, but this time it was as if my sudden optimism began to spread to her like pollen on the air. Little things – the fact that I seemed to be writing actual letters and putting them in actual envelopes and walking them to the actual post office – put a blush back in her cheeks.

— Am I allowed to know to whom you were sending these letters?

— Of course. But I simply wanted to start by saying that our plan—

— Your plan.

— My plan has already begun to pay off. I think even the girls are perking up – they sense the mood in the house, you know. They're walking polygraph machines. The point is I'm doing this for my family, and it's working.

— Which means you've taken step two and stopped seeing – can't remember . . . Sophie, was it?

— Give me time, Saddler. It's only been six weeks. At this stage Sophie's still an asset. Trust me, it's about the least emotional relationship one could imagine. Some people go to the cinema to watch actors pretend to do this; I actually do it. I'm going to guess you know exactly what I'm talking about where . . . detached physical love is concerned.

— Don't assume too much.

— Come off it. Anyway, I practise on Sophie, I train on her, and any time now this new fitness and skill will be brought back to the home ground. Least of my worries.

— You're so cold. I'll let that pass. I need a report.

— All right. I decided to start with the Vatican.

— I must have been *very* drunk to have agreed to this deal. God, my palms have been sweating ever since the moment we shook hands. I'd been listening to you, thinking you were talking about some little . . . curiosity. Clever of you to have held out for so long on the value of the thing – if you're right about that. When you said the word "million", I must have thought it was a joke. I'd been thinking in the order of a year's school fees, a tiding-over sum. I've been spending all this time hoping you'd been kidding yourself, that you'd reconsidered. But you haven't, have you?

— No. And the reason – relax, Saddler – the reason I began with the Vatican was to have some sort of authentic, actually intimidating interest, first of all, then use that as ammunition when I approached the crazy collectors. I sat on park benches and practised my spiel, my *pitch*. I thought of the scene: clip-clopping down an endless parquet hall, a quartet of plumed-helmeted Swiss Guards on each side of me, pope portraits staring power-madly down, a crimson-beenied cardinal on a throne appearing in the far distance, the guards dismissed, the cardinal's cadaver voice asking me, "Where did you get the map?" The moment I replied, "That's not important," or, "Later, Monsignor. In good time," or any variation on these cover-ups, I imagined the clang of iron gates and the return of the guards and the dance of the candelabra flames as I was frog-marched to the dungeon.

— My nightmare exactly.

— This just shows how little we know about today's Vatican. Here's what happened. I wrote to old Andreas, who's married now, has two little girls as I do, lives in Munich, still dabbles in the business but runs a connoisseur's whisky bar to make ends meet.

— Did he ever sell on the Hawaii?

— Hah. He's hung it on the wall behind the bar. Said he wanted to make a dartboard out of it. No, the Hawaii's worthless as ever.

— Wasn't he suspicious about your writing to him, out of the blue? People don't write letters anymore, do they?

— I do. Andreas knows I hate computers. I wrote a friendly, casual letter. I told him about my new job with Rory, whom he knows. And I simply asked him for the name of his cardinal acquaintance, making it sound as if Rory were the one interested. And so I got the name of Cardinal Schumm, and the man's Rome address.

— He lives in Rome?

— Half of the time. Andreas has known Schumm since university days, when Schumm was a youngish lecturer on German literature. Schumm seemed like a normal guy, like Andreas interested in art history, then freaked out after his mother's very bizarre suicide and got back into the Church in an extremely serious way. He appeared to be sincere, but one can't help thinking what an absolute dream job it would be to climb the rungs of an organisation like that. The travel, the perks, the iron-clad employment security.

— The *clothes*, my dear. The *slippers*.

— I know, and adorable nuns to bring up the tea. I'm not saying this was Schumm's motivation, of course. But one gathers that Europe is thirsting for priests in the first place, and here was university-educated, socially at ease, good-looking, erudite, well-spoken, multilingual Schumm who probably looked like pope material the day he took holy orders. His mother, I should add, was a divorcee environmental activist who had a history of chaining herself to corporate headquarters, lying down on train tracks in the path of nuclear waste, exposing her mastectomy scars in front of embassies. Frau Schumm killed herself in the most appalling way. You don't want to know.

— . . .

— OK. She gathered some press, made sure cameras were rolling. She gave a short anti-war speech, not specifying *which* war, but it was assumed she meant Vietnam or maybe Nicaragua. She mentioned those Saigon monks. Before anyone could stop her she made herself into a human Molotov cocktail. Took a swig of petrol, flicked the lighter, *whoosh*.

— Doesn't sound very Catholic. Nor German, for that matter. How could I not have heard?

— It was suppressed. It wasn't considered sufficiently political, I suppose. Private madness. Anyway, this is the tragedy that propelled young Schumm into the bosom of Mother Church, where he has thrived ever since. He is a senior member of the Arts and Antiquities Acquisition Committee, Vatican, Rome, Italy.

— *Wunderbar*.

— I received a reply on the most divine stationery – some sort of raised *velour* for the heading, I swear to God. Cardinal

Schumm would be pleased to make time for me, in Rome.

— You couldn't very well bring the map, though.

— Of course not. I photographed it, weighed it and measured it. I put together what documentation I could find.

— Where is the map physically kept?

— In a false-bottomed drawer in my desk at home.

— Wouldn't a bank be better?

— I don't *have* a bank, in that sense. Every map of mine is sold, every one. If I ever got back in the business –

— Of course you will.

— – I'll be starting from scratch. In the meantime, if someone wants to steal my already hot map, good luck to them. The cardinal knew he and his people weren't going to see the physical object. So I packed a light bag, flew to Rome, taxied to the Vatican.

— By this time I'd be on the verge of a stroke. How nervous were you?

— Not at all, Saddler. Beyond nerves. Acting out a role. Looking out of the taxi window at all the other crooks. I didn't expect much to come of the meeting. I just needed to be able to say, "I've spoken to the Vatican," when the time came to meet my crazies later. What could Schumm do? What power did he really have? What would a man sitting on a zillion in art all over the world want with my shiny little map? That was my frame of mind when I walked in there. I hadn't been to the Vatican since I was a child. I had the driver drop me at the gates so I could walk with purpose across St Peter's Square. It would make a better story if I told you I went straight up the steps and was met by a colourful guard, and so on, but when I asked for directions I discovered that Schumm's offices were what they call "extraterritorial", that is to say, back out in smoky Rome. I'm saying I didn't exactly enjoy a papal audience. Schumm wanted to meet on the third floor of a modern office block. The person who greeted me in reception was a young American priest – so far, so Catholic, I suppose.

Except where you'd want the distant echo of the drip-drip of holy water on millenary stone, that sort of thing, I found myself in a stuffy office, two women stationed at computers, not so much as a crucifix in sight. The young American, who wanted me to call him Father Anthony, was the only authentic element. I'd wanted whispering in cloisters, a couple of stooped monks trimming hedges and looking madly over their shoulders in fear of the new arrival, and I got what looked like a small-town travel agent's.

— Cardinals have to work this way?

— Evidently some of them do. Perhaps back home they are treated better. Schumm appeared, alone, a few minutes later. Again, one expected trumpet fanfares, a swirl of crimson vestments—

— The hiss of slippers on marble.

— Yes. Instead, a shattered-looking senior priest, wearing standard-issue black and white. He was a tall, ruddy fellow. He had unusual bushy blond hair like straight wire and huge reddish eyebrows. He spoke American English. I wanted to say, "You're a *cardinal*?"

— I suppose we only see them in their Sunday best. How disappointing.

— His office was slightly more what we might have hoped. At least they'd given him a grand old desk. Father Anthony left us. I was able to break the ice – and to establish my credentials somewhat – by knowing about and remarking upon most of the objects he'd put on display here and there. The maps were all old copies, but that's appropriate. Austro-Hungarian stuff. Schumm said he didn't have much time, which I doubted because his shoes were unpolished, his soft briefcase looked empty, and quite frankly he smelled. I said I would be brief, and went into my rehearsed pitch. A map had come into the possession of someone who had entrusted me with its sale. It wasn't important who that person was. It was one of those fortuitous finds that people like me won't see twice in a lifetime. I gently flattered him about

Andreas' immediate recommendation of his good name. I said I knew he was a busy man, but that he ought to take a careful look at what I was about to show him. There were going to be a lot of collectors interested, I said. At this point he stopped me and said that, in any case, a number of his expert associates would inevitably be called in, if we got past his preliminary judgement. I said of course that would be the case. This was a treasure. I said I couldn't wait to show him what I had, but that I needed his word beforehand that no matter his opinion, whether we proceeded to the next step or not, I wanted his word that he would not discuss the nature of the map with anyone not directly involved in its acquisition. He very solemnly agreed to these terms. I think he liked me.

— Oh? He didn't ask, "Where did you steal this map?"

— Strangely, no. He seemed relaxed. He didn't even want to know why I didn't send the thing straight to free auction. I asked him, as I was opening my briefcase, if he dealt in a lot of maps in his official capacity, or if that were more of a private activity. He reminded me that he'd taken a vow of poverty. I said I hadn't known, and I apologised for my ignorance. He added that maps were a great love of his, and that he'd been privileged since having been appointed to the committee to see a number of stunning examples of the craft. I took out my magnifying glass and the first photograph, and slid them to the centre of his desk. "Well, then," I said to him.

— The sheer drama, Hart.

— Absolutely. Now the big German strapped on a pair of spectacles – vow-of-poverty specs, I might add, they could have been salvaged from a plane crash. I really thought, if this chap's going to be pope some day, they'll have to thoroughly tart him up. He seized the magnifying glass, then handled the photo as if it were the engraving itself. I had prepared myself not to say anything at this moment, though I wanted to. I sat back and crossed my arms. The cardinal squinted through the magnifying glass. He held the print up to the natural light from the window. Have I mentioned how loud it was in his office? Not a room for the contemplative man, what with the traffic noises and the sirens. I began to feel sorry for Cardinal Schumm, as I studied his face and searched it for a reaction to my map. He squinted, he frowned, he looked the photo up and down. He turned the print this way and that, presumably to make out the microscopic text. This went on for so long that I couldn't stand the tension anymore. I sat forward and began to say that I'd brought along a number of interesting documents that would help him place the map in context – but he held up and splayed the fingers that had been gripping the magnifying glass, silencing me.

— This is good. He was interested in what he'd seen. This *was* good, wasn't it?

— Seemed so to me. He wouldn't let me speak, but he accepted each document, one by one, as I gently passed them across his desk. I nudged them over in ascending order of interest. My trump card was a series of overlays I had drawn of the various Compostela pilgrim routes. For a pilgrim site to put itself on the map, so to speak, it helped to have a crusade pass through and, preferably, to have a crusader die there only to be canonised later on. My map suggested at least two such places. Plain as day. As I told you, one of these towns was St-Vuis, then known as Visso. The other is what's now called Court d'Haleine, where I've never been. It's just a village down in the Pyrenees, not even a tourist spot, despite the joke name.

— Why would a village want a joke name?

— The story goes that the village – I'm talking about a thousand years ago – grandly named itself Court d'Helène, hoping to expand by virtue of this phoney association. The scheme never took. The village had built a church atop their miserable hill, reachable only by exactly one thousand steps. Thus, short of breath. Thus, Court d'Haleine. But according to my map there may have been a time when Compostela pilgrims took all those steps as part of their journey of penance and enlightenment.

— Go back for a moment. You took this map because of St-Vuis, didn't you?

— Well, the name certainly leaped out at me. Yes, I suppose you're right. If I hadn't seen that name, I might not have been so struck by the map, nor suddenly so criminally minded again.

— And you were hoping the cardinal was going to want this map for publicity value more than anything else.

— I imagine they're looking at ways to galvanise the flock, wouldn't you think so? Not least in France. With good evidence they could swiftly shine a light on those two towns and the next thing you know, tens of thousands would be passing out from dehydration on the thousand steps of Court d'Haleine, or causing traffic problems for Cambon's colleagues in St-Vuis. It's the weeping-Virgin syndrome. It happens all the time that one mayor or another, strapped for cash, will discover a Virgin weeping blood in the local church. Next thing you know you're on American telly and two summers later the new school is paid for.

— The Church has to think long term.

— That's what I say. Imagine it – you're in the top three or four religions in the whole world. If one in a thousand Catholics takes an interest in a new cult phenomenon – bingo, a million people march on St-Vuis and Court d'Haleine.

— If they can afford it.

— Afford it? Have you ever *seen* a pilgrim? They'd find a way to walk there from the Cape of Good Hope. Anyway, I imagined all of this would be racing through Cardinal Schumm's mind as he inspected the map and read my documentation and traced with his index finger the unimaginably fine lines of the lost pilgrim routes.

— Who were those lunatics, anyway?

— Saddler, you must never be cynical about the Middle Ages. And besides, there are far more pilgrims today than there were eight hundred years ago. If you include the hajj, well, need I say more? If I'd been born in, say, 1198, I can assure you I'd be crawling on my hands and knees to Jerusalem. What's more important is what pilgrims represent – and the stunning, fantastic, against-all-odds endurance of Christianity might very well pay off my mortgage and send my children to reasonably good schools.

— Ah. Schumm liked it.

— Schumm's a cagey sort. He'd done this before. You don't shout "Eureka!" and open the Vatican cash vault. And, by the way, their money isn't in the Vatican, or even in Italy. Vatican wealth comes in the form of real estate, mostly. Don't try to think about every Catholic-owned building, church, cathedral – it'll make you sick. I'm no expert, but I knew that if Schumm showed an interest in my map he wouldn't be offering cash, or not enough. The sum I had in mind would have to go all the way to the top. They would have to find a wealthy benefactor to buy the map in the Church's name. Not long ago it would have been old man Kennedy. Can you tell me where they've gone, the billionaire Catholics?

— Mafia?

— You said it, Saddler, I didn't. The cardinal looked kosher to me, though. If he wanted this treasure, and if he thought the way I did about the pilgrim-value of such an object – and, crucially, if his experts agreed with me that the thing was authentic – he would find the money. You mentioned the Church's long-term view. My great hope was that Schumm would see right through me, understand that the map was hot as Hades, not mention this, wire a million and a half to Switzerland, and arrange to keep the map's existence secret for, say, three hundred years, by which time its trail would have gone ice cold. Or at least he would wait until after my death.

— What have been your thoughts about money laundering? I've never understood how that's done.

— With the greatest insouciance, I gather. Buy a house in Spain, half cash under the table? Leak the money into a business?

In my case, slowly buy more maps with cash? How far would a million go, anyway, if I permanently had a stash of notes in my briefcase? I see myself taking frequent trips to Lac Léman with the family, or whatever's closest to Liechtenstein, crossing the border on the return trip with ten or fifty thousand stashed with the passports in the glove box. You must know plenty of people who do this.

— One or two. No, you're right, more than that. And they're quite open about it. They say, "Think of the trillions in drugs and arms money, groaning in Swiss vaults, sluicing about the world. Harmful money. Mine's a nest egg for the children, hard earned by honest labour."

— Exactly. Except, in our case, for the honest labour.

— You haven't told me Schumm's verdict yet, and we're already buying houses for cash in Spain.

— He's a serious man, Schumm. Rather a sad look to him. Dandruff, a curse for the man who must wear black. But when he took off those specs and looked at me, I knew I had him. "Mr Davies," he said—

— Oh, Hart. No.

— Was I supposed to go under my real name?

— I was wondering what you'd done to your hair.

— And I was waiting for you to mention it. I experimented with a bottle of Mary's highlighting stuff. When I came out of the shower looking like a tropical fish, I told her I'd mistaken the bottle for normal shampoo.

— In a very disconcerting way, it suits you.

— It's grown out. You should have seen me in Rome. I looked like a sorbet ice cream cone. I think Father Anthony wanted to take me back to his quarters.

— So you were Mr Davies. Presumably Andreas introduced you that way to the cardinal?

— Yes, on the pretext that I didn't want my Vatican deal to get mixed up with my work for Rory Fine.

— Not that I've ever given much thought to subterfuge, but isn't one of the basic rules not to set too many lies in train? To stick as close to the truth as possible? You can lose track of lies. I believe the expression goes, "They'll catch up with you."

— I know all that. There are only two lies so far: that I have been authorised to sell the map, and that my name is Philip Davies. I can keep track of those.

— OK, then. Where did you leave things with Cardinal Schumm?

— He didn't exactly *gush*, but I could tell he'd never seen anything quite like my map. He said he would arrange for two experts to see the real thing, in London, within the next few weeks. I was going to insist that these experts not be English, lest I be known to them, but before I did so the cardinal said his experts were French and Spanish. I collected my photos and documents; we shook hands; I was shown out by Father Anthony. I came home the same day. Mary never knew I'd left London.

— So I guess you're satisfied with your first stab at this project?

— Hmm, yes. You know one of the things I love about you, Saddler?

— What could that be?

— That you could sit here for however long it's been and not mention that I look like a Guatemalan macaw. Do you have to practise, to be so cool?

— I was brought up not to make personal remarks.

— Let me get us another round.

— . . .

— Mustn't let me drink too much this time, Saddler. I have to visit Sophie this evening.

— That's unfair.

— Unfair? *Unfair?* And I suppose you won't be having your way with someone you've never met behind a south-of-the-river club?

— I meant unfair to Mary. Your *wife*.

— Easy for you to say. You live in another moral dimension.

With whom will you be passionate later on? Do you know yet? Or will you try to give the old loins a rest?

— You assume too much.

— Oh, do I?

— As a matter of fact, I'm painting my flat. I'm selling.

— That's big news, Saddler. Are you sure it's a good idea? Once you fall off the ladder . . .

— Well, since we're being businessmen now, I suppose if I said I'll probably see a three-hundred-per-cent return over six years, you might recognise the wisdom in this decision. Besides, I need the money for the French properties. I'm ridiculously exposed down there.

— Where will you live?

— First I'll buy a smaller flat in London, some ruin, probably way, way out west somewhere, maybe back to my roots in Kew. I'll have that made liveable while I stay at what you call my chateau and pay attention to the two other festering pieces of shit I own down there. Any money that comes my way from your scheme goes straight into the chateau, mostly the fucking gardens. Something very strange is going on with the climate in the South of France. One year you think, well, why not, a stand of palms. When those are wiped out you think, well, I'm lucky to have a few drops of water, let's give the fruit orchard a go. When the glacier recedes, you think again. Sane people just plant lavender, photograph it for posterity in a good year, and pray.

— Sorry to hear that. I didn't know you had two other properties. I thought it was just the one you were trying to flog.

— The other two are nearby, practically neighbours to one another. Would you like one? You may be able to afford it soon. It might be just the thing if you don't mind this new screaming wind we've got which makes the Mistral feel like a lulling tropical zephyr. Did you say you wanted electricity? Comes with, sort of. Keep your children away from the light switches. There's very little upkeep on either of these places, if you adore weeds and not just dead but rotten, stinking, putrefied ex-vines.

— Why on earth did you buy these places?

— Because, ten years ago, they looked marvellous. I turned my back, waiting for them to appreciate, and it's as if an evil spell has been cast upon them. I hadn't been back to one of them for about two years and, when I did visit, a roof had collapsed and somehow great milky vines had crawled out towards the sky and neck-high thorn bushes had completely overgrown the place where the kitchen used to be. I hacked my way in there, and with that bitch wind whipping my face over the crumbled walls, I burst into tears.

— You never told me any of this.

— Well, first of all I never seem to get a word in, and second of all I honestly prefer to suffer alone. What I mean is, it's embarrassing. Everyone used to say, "Darius has certainly made a life for himself, mincing about his French properties choosing floor tiles and stone sinks and rose beds, such a perfectly *gay* life – and the divine Antoine!" And now, a snap of the fingers later, I'm reviled for the Sam business; Antoine, as we speak, is sucking off some great greasy pig on the Adriatic; one of my French properties is lying there in the boiling wind like the bombed-out Reichstag; and I'm painting the walls of my own flat *myself*, like some arse-crack skivvy.

— Poor Saddler.

— I hope you think it's noble of me, then, to have absorbed all of your information without a word until now, the same way I refrained from mentioning your ridiculous hair. But don't let me stop you. I'm sure there's more.

— Well, I ought to report that I got tough with my blackmailer. Or I tried to. He upped his price again, and I decided, for the first time, not to pay. I didn't tell him this. I simply didn't deliver the envelope. He wanted five hundred this time. If he called me back I was going to say I didn't have the money. I was going to stall.

Not only did he get back to me, he did so within a few hours of not finding the envelope where he'd demanded I make the drop.

— Did he threaten you?

— Not exactly. You know, his voice seems to be different every time. At first, as I told you, it was a terrible mockney, which gradually became more northern, gruff and matey, then it swirled over to Ireland. This time he sounded like a very disappointed prep-school headmaster, quite low and jowly. The scary thing was, he knew more about my experience in St-Vuis than he had before. He knew details. "You naughty little wanker," he said. No, I wouldn't call that threatening. If anything he seemed to take pity on me. He knew Annette's name. He even knew I'd been staring at the girl in the restaurant the night before she died.

— So Cambon's been blabbing.

— Or the girl's parents. The blackmailer said I should call him Porter. He spoke of himself in the third person. He said, "I know you're starting to think, maybe Porter's bluffing. Maybe old Porter wouldn't go to the red tops with your disgusting little story." He asked me if I'd read about the BA navigator who was photographed drinking and participating in an orgy in Crete just six hours before a flight.

— I read about that.

— Porter said, "He was one of mine." I asked him how many people he was blackmailing – we were discussing this very matter-of-factly. He said, "I'm running three dozen of you blokes at the moment." It's an excellent scam. He catches people misbehaving abroad, where they think they'll get away with it, and as soon as they come home Porter's all over them. He has some "domestic cases" as well. He named names. You and I would never have heard of these people – they're on television, or they play football. "Footy alone," Porter said, "could keep me in business full time." He said something I found rather clever. He said he could pick a footballer at random, ring him up, accuse him of having an extramarital affair, and start the blackmail then and there without any evidence. "They are all, without exception, at it." Porter just cold-calls people, known or not, completely out of the blue, accuses them of misbehaviour, gets a breathless "How did you know?" on the other end, and blackmails them. If you extrapolate from what Porter told me, there must be very few people left in Britain who aren't being blackmailed one way or another.

— How long are you expected to go along with this?

— I asked Porter that question. He said he normally runs a person like me for five years. Or until the blackmailee confesses to his loved ones, whichever comes first.

— So all you have to do is tell Mary, and Porter will go away?

— Ah. Mary. Hasn't it already occurred to you that it's very likely Mary who's behind this whole thing? It's her revenge. Only she knew most of the things Porter knows. The others, she could have had Porter track down. But I'll be one step ahead of her. I'll lay traps. I've already been paying blackmail for nine months now. If I told Mary, and it turned out she *wasn't* orchestrating the whole business, it would look like I've had something to hide. Mary would want to know how things stand, and I'd have to tell her Cambon suspects me of having killed the girl.

— What?

— He has no other suspects. I was there, I was staring at her, her body was found right outside my hotel window; I was . . . doing what I was doing. What is he supposed to think? Cambon said as much to me. Like the blackmailer, he rings me on my mobile.

— Maybe he and Porter are working together?

— That's occurred to me. It's certainly possible, but not as likely as Mary being the culprit. She has the motivation of having started to hate me. But what better scheme than to work with coppers all over the Continent, getting the names of our countrymen who've done things they'd rather not have widely known. Porter says he's got MPs in his pocket, fat cats, and so on. "My bread and butter," he said, "is the little man, like you."

— We have to find out who Porter is. You should just have it out with Mary.

— Now that Porter has become so talkative, I've tried to find clues in the things he says. His voice and his accent are all over the map. The people he's blackmailing are from every part of the country. The way to get to him, obviously, would be to ask the journalists he leaks his stories to.

— Great idea.

— I tried it. I rang up the reporter who wrote about the BA navigator. I put on my best Glasgow accent and said, "Look, I'm being blackmailed over a minor indiscretion, and the fellow who's blackmailing me is the one who gave you the navigator-drunk-orgy story, so be a good chap and tell me his name." Surprisingly, the reporter wanted to help. One has the impression that these desperadoes who work at the tabloids are creatures of the night – you know, feral and slimy, sell their own mothers for dirt on a junior minister. But this young man was very polite and well spoken. He was appropriately self-hating for the job he did. He said he disliked the idea that private people like me were being jerked around by a blackmailer. He stood by his navigator story, because the navigator was obviously putting lives at risk by drinking raki until sunrise and then getting into the cockpit of a commercial airliner. He asked me what I'd done that I didn't want known. I told him I'd had a one-night stand with a Spanish waitress. "We wouldn't print that," he said. "No offence," he said, "but who'd give a toss? Unless you're married and famous, that is." So I had to make my story more interesting.

— For God's sake, Hart, why?

— I don't know. Maybe I *was* offended. What did he mean, my extramarital fling with a *señorita* wasn't news? Because I was "a little man"? No, I had to make the story better because otherwise he'd just tell me to tell Porter to bugger off: he had no basis for blackmail if the tabloids weren't interested. So I thickened my fake accent and told him I'd roughed up the girl, who turned out to be Pablo Picasso's granddaughter by a hitherto unknown liaison in the 60s. He became interested and wanted to ask me questions. But here, Saddler, is where I began to think deviously. You're going to be proud of me. I do believe I'm turning into one of those people who is capable of playing and winning the game. Here's what I did: I suggested to the journalist that no story the blackmailer gave him was ever going to be as big as the story of the blackmailer himself. Do you follow me? If we could somehow bust the Porter character, find out how many people he's running, and who they are, it would be one of the biggest stories of the year. Blackmail is illegal. A mischievous man calling himself Porter claims to be blackmailing dozens of people, many of whom are publicly known. Others, more poignantly, are "little men", like me. And here's where I really poured on the logic. If I'd now told the journalist that his source for scandalous stories was in fact a rampant blackmailer – if the journalist now *knew* this – he couldn't very well carry on printing what Porter told him. He would be complicit in blackmail. I suggested he might have to tell his editor. I suggested that together we could entrap the blackmailer . . . And this is where my logic ran out.

— Why? It was all making sense to me.

— Well, Saddler, the whole point of blackmail is that the victim doesn't want his secret told. If I helped trap Porter, he would only raise the stakes. The journalist pointed out this flaw right away. He really seemed to be on my side. He told me that if he somehow managed to discover the blackmailer's identity, all it would mean was that my having roughed up Picasso's granddaughter would be out in the open. He couldn't sit on that story, he said. He added that during our conversation my accent seemed to have headed considerably south of Glasgow.

— Has it occurred to you yet that you might not be *perfectly* suited to the world of intrigue?

— There is that possibility. The fact is I suddenly found myself backtracking and begging the journalist to forget I'd ever mentioned the blackmailer, that I hadn't raped anyone, that Porter didn't even exist, that I was a mentally unbalanced attention seeker. That's how our conversation ended.

— Points for trying, Hart. Perhaps you ought to keep things simple from now on?

— At least I was calling from a public telephone. One of the precautions one learns to take. This was on a street corner at lunchtime, two down from Rory's building. I'll have to go ahead and confess that about fifteen minutes into my chat with the journalist, Rory himself wandered by, saw me, came over, made a "Have time for a drink?" gesture, and when I smiled encouragingly he waited there watching me deal with the journalist. He had that conspiratorial fellow-adulterer's smirk on his face. None but a criminal or a cheat would use a call box in London anymore. When I emerged from the box, I plucked my mobile phone from my pocket and said, "Dead battery." At which moment my mobile rang.

— You have all the luck.

— I went off with Rory for that drink, making all sorts of excuses, cursing the unpredictable mobile. I had half a mind to let Rory in on the Stenniman map. Maybe he'd help?

— Please say you didn't.

— I didn't. He's a wonderful man, Rory, but too successful at the moment to want to get involved in something like that. He lies and steals in a more conventional way. He's my age, but when we're together I feel like his apprentice. Or his nephew, perhaps, in the Big Smoke for a day trip to see the sights. Rory is such a giant, really, in the sense that he seems to draw pleasure from every second of every day, barrelling along and never looking over his shoulder at the turbulence he's caused. His only fear is terrorism. He's convinced London is next, that London is overdue. He doesn't fear for his safety, mind you. He fears for his business. He's afraid his treasures will be poisoned by radiation.

I had to remind him that my own career was partially destroyed by terrorism.

— I didn't know that.

— Oh, yes. It was just before the fiasco with the Hawaii. My girls were tiny. I felt I was doing well. That next sale was going to have me in clover. I was going to parlay that success into something more along the lines of what Rory does – you know, open up my own house. I still had grand ideas. And one of the springboards was going to be media exposure. Do you think I'd be presentable on television?

— I'd say you were *born* for television.

— Thank you. It happens that I'd been invited to go on radio to talk about a map-forgery case. Perhaps you remember it?

— No.

— You would have, if it hadn't been for terrorism. Millions in fake maps, poisoning the market, forger identified, expert – that would be me – called in for a full Beeb hour to talk about the ins and outs of the rare-map world, making a name, shaking the important hands, eye contact. Next stop? A telly broadcast. That's how I saw the future. A nice four-part documentary, rushing about the world, explaining maps, making a lot of money, getting known, hanging out my shingle and living the rest of my life rich and contented. Such was my optimistic mood on September 11, 2001, as I chatted with a sound man in a studio in Bush House, ready for the interview. We were, I swear to God, ten minutes away from going on the air, and that . . . that *thing* started happening over in New York. There I was with my lips an inch away from the microphone, with the interviewer and her assistant and the sound man, ready to become famous. Seconds later I was watching a monitor along with everyone else, and while they were gasping and scurrying about and making fruitless phone calls to find out if they knew anyone who was dying, I was still muttering, "My interview, my interview . . ." Obviously it was the most shocking and tragic event one had ever seen, but on top of their primary crimes those terrorist pricks completely fucked up my career that day.

— If they'd struck two months earlier I would have lost the sale of a house. These were Americans, and they probably wouldn't have taken the flight over.

— A narrow escape for you, then. By the time the dust had settled, the Beeb were no longer interested in what I had to say about map forgery. Those terrorists had a lot to answer for. How I cheered on the American war machine! Every cruise missile was a blow of revenge for me, personally. I was strongly in favour of a total invasion of the entire Arabian peninsula, never mind piss-ant Afghanistan. Some people think the Americans overreacted – are they *kidding*? Who's going to bring back my radio interview, my television documentary, my antique-map boutique right across the street from Rory Fine's? And invading Iraq was the stupidest thing anyone's ever done. Iraq should have been our staunchest ally against the Saudis, the Yemenis – secularise the lot of them under one great, pitiless, pan-Arab dictator.

— I've never known you to be political.

— This isn't political, this is personal. It's my *life* those warped, inadequate, *mother*fucking lunatics destroyed. If you'd lost the sale of that house to the Americans, you wouldn't be such a lily-livered peacenik.

— Who said I was? Let them have all the wars they want. I have an out-of-control garden that needs seeing to. I have books I'd like to sit down quietly and read. Perhaps there's even a great love in my future, who knows?

— That's more like it. Let's allow the wider world to get on with its struggles, and pay more attention to our own fulfilment. We don't have long on this earth, so let's have another drink and I'll tell you about the first of my crazy collectors.

— . . .

— Cheers, Saddler.

— Cheers.

— So. The first collector on my list is the scariest. I thought I'd start with him because it's always been my policy to perform the most unpleasant tasks first. All of my dealings after Manny Horstedt were going to be a blessed relief. I'd never met him before, but everyone in my business has known about Manny Horstedt for decades. He's called "Horstedt the Hoarder". Like a substantial minority of truly obsessive collectors, he combines inherited wealth with the mildest and most useful autism. This plays into the hands of dealers, because once Manny has his strangely wired brain set on an object, it will be his. He can't rest until he owns it and has it lined up in a clean display case, ordered chronologically, catalogued to the nth degree. The only doubt I had was whether or not my silver map fitted in with his collection, preferably in a gaping hole he would not rest until he'd filled. Another reason to start with Manny is that he lives in London. Like any sensible Swede a generation or two ago, he moved here for tax reasons. Then he fell in love with the place – to the extent that someone who never leaves his house can fall in love with a city – and didn't go home even when the financial climate improved. It's hard to say how wealthy he is, but the sources are the usual suspects from his part of the world: steel, pharmaceuticals, lumber. It's safe to assume that Mad Manny is sitting on a conservatively invested eighty to one hundred million pounds, making him moderately wealthy even by London standards.

— You are *such* a bitch.

— People like Manny, especially if they're Scandinavian, are usually called reclusive and miserly. You know, they travel economy class and drive pre-war cars and knit their own socks. They're supposed to sit in stuffy rooms with the curtains drawn, puzzling over hundred-year-old chess matches. They ferment their own wine from berries they pick on the verges of motorways.

— You're going to tell me that's all a stereotype, and Mad

Manny's a freewheeling playboy who has his own jet and enjoys only the finest vintages.

— No. He's a reclusive, miserly depressive: he doesn't socialise, he doesn't drive, he sits in a stuffy room with the curtains drawn studying chess and drinking berry wine his wife brews in the cellar. He's not just a stereotype, he's the archetype. He has a long-suffering English wife, Martha, whom he treats like a slave, and two grown, disinherited sons who live in the Far East. He's in his mid-sixties.

— He doesn't sound like a mood-improving man.

— I wore black to our first meeting. His reply to my long letter was, in full, "Five pm, 16th," written in a woman's hand. He must have dictated this to his wife from the shadows of his dank study. I threw caution to the wind and brought the map with me. I'd bought a black velvet sleeve to add a bit of glamour to the object. Manny has lived in the same house in St Alban's Grove since the day he arrived in London more than thirty years ago. I took the Tube to Kensington High Street, emerged into beautiful, clear evening sun, and walked south. As soon as I turned into Manny's street, the sky darkened. As I walked the hundred yards to his address, the gloom descended to black. A horrid rain began to fall. I paused at the gate of Manny's tall house. The strip of front garden looked like an overgrown cemetery. The formerly white facade was pitted and stained. Some of the windows were cracked, and behind each one was a black shade.

— You turned and fled?

— I opened the rusty gate, climbed the crumbling steps, tried the broken doorbell, knocked. I was glad I had dressed as an undertaker. The door creaked open and there stood Martha – petite, well coifed, dressed as if for a philanthropists' awards ceremony, smiling apologetically. I wanted to grab her hand and shout, "Run, Martha, run!" Instead I let her guide me into the sepulchre.

— I'm so glad you're *living* for a change.

— I could tell right away that the house was divided into two parts: Martha's and Manny's. On the left of the entrance hall was a clean, bright kitchen. On the right, where Martha led me, was gloom and rough dark wood and an atmosphere of death. Martha knocked on a tall, heavy door, opened it without waiting for a reply, gestured for me to enter the room, then backed away and shut me inside.

— Spooky.

— Manny Horstedt rose from an armchair in the darkest, furthest corner of the cavernous room. The place stank of old parchment. It was hot and humid in there; it felt somehow *pressurised.* I approached the man and kept my voice low as I introduced myself. You'd imagine that a guy with Manny's reputation, who lived in a room like that, would look like a desiccated cadaver, that he would have crooked, rotting teeth, that from a distance one could smell disease on his breath, that he would wear bedroom slippers, that he would stare madly and blindly through bottle-thick glasses.

— You're going to tell me he turned out to be the opposite – a tall, fresh-faced, youthful man with a springy step and all the social graces he was heir to.

— No. The former, to a T. A walking tragedy, exactly as I described. He was so frail, I felt the urge to take his elbow with my left hand as I clasped his brittle fingers with my right. "We'll go to my desk," he said. He took short, trembling steps across the room. He could have been thirty years older than his actual age. Breathing in and out seemed to sap half his energy. It made one rethink wanting to be rich. Or at least, rethink wishing that one had inherited wealth. I had the strongest feeling that it wasn't poor health or mental illness that had crippled this man and put him for ever in a dark room: it was not knowing what to do with his money.

— Oh my, dear me, yes, how frightfully *stifling*.

— You scoff, as usual, but maybe what I have to say next will change your tune. The thing is, after twenty minutes with Manny I felt that we were close friends. I hadn't even mentioned the map yet. Martha had come in with an unlabelled bottle of berry wine and two plastic tumblers. Manny, seated behind his desk, began to "defend" – his word – some of the objects in his cupboards and cabinets. He had a strong Swedish accent still. He spoke slowly and precisely. God knows what his physical ailments were, but his mind was focused and clear – in an extremely narrow way. The arrangement of his features didn't really allow him to smile, but his eyes, magnified by those thick glasses, expressed the great, single-minded joy of a collector's collector. That's what I was trying to say, just now. He'd been a wealthy man since his parents' early deaths when he was twenty. He'd looked out at the world and decided he had always loved old maps. It wasn't a hobby, it wasn't a job, it wasn't mere diversion. It was everything. He went deeper and deeper into the only thing he cared about, and blotted out the rest with black window shades. We think obsessive gardeners are adorable, we think poets are inspired, we think doctors – like my brother – are saints. So who are we to judge Mad Manny, when for all we know he's having a more profound experience of life than all of them, while most of us just flail about in search of random moments of happiness?

— I admire your empathy. The man sounds loopy.

— You're cruel, Saddler. I'm telling you, I felt a great surge of *love* for the old guy. He'd harmed no one, ever, in his life. Not even Martha, as I could tell by the way she looked at him. Manny was *her* life. We're all different, Saddler. That was their way.

— I thought you said you weren't going to drink too much. You've gone all soft in the head.

— Am I not allowed to show a little honest emotion? Manny had me stand up and tour his collection, pointing things out from his chair. All right, maybe he is a touch on the autistic side. I asked him about security – just the treasures I saw, the ones on display, were worth – God, seriously, Saddler, millions. Millions.

I had to bite my tongue not to suggest I sell some maps for him – he's never sold a single map, ever, in his whole life. He said the security was "fine", and I noticed that the inside of the door I'd come through had one of those submarine-chamber-lock wheels. Manny's only household improvement, it seemed, was a system to seal off that room. He didn't believe in alarms. He believed in living inside a vault. "I sleep right there," he said. There was a prison-style cot beneath the one window, which was heavily barred. I imagine Martha came in to give him a sponge bath now and then.

— So having fallen in love with this kook, you unsleeved your map.

— I asked Manny's permission to adjust his desk lamp. I got out my magnifying glass. And, yes, I put on a pair of white-cotton gloves and placed a second pair on the desk for Manny. These things have to be done properly.

— May I interrupt for just a second to ask you a question?

— Go ahead.

— You don't really, honestly know what your map is worth – true?

— My map, Saddler, is worth exactly what the highest bidder is willing to pay.

— But you don't know. You don't have a *reserve*.

— I have an inkling. I have a hunch. These are backed up by a certain amount of hard-earned expertise, thank you very much. You think I'm desperate, that I'm taking a punt.

— We shall see, I suppose.

— We certainly shall, if you'd let me continue.

— Carry on, then.

— Manny's body gave out the most awful *cracking* sound as he leaned forward and donned the gloves. His hands trembled – Parkinson's? Too much berry wine? Not *enough* berry wine? He began to open the velvet sleeve, then stopped and asked me to "put on the gramophone". I hadn't seen a turntable in ten years.

It took me a moment to remember how to work the thing. I put the needle down at the beginning of the record that was already lying there. Now, what sort of music do you think a person like Mad Manny would listen to, alone in his dark room?

— I'd wager something ethereal, something to take him away from the world. That would be . . . well, Beethoven, of course. One of those quartets the eggheads get so excited about.

— Nice try. It was big-band jazz. At volume. A first release, from the sound of the scratches. Manny croaked the name Ellington over the music. Even I knew who that was. I took a moment to flick through Manny's old records, and they were all American jazz bands.

— That's all Nathan ever listened to, as well. He said he could close his eyes and be dancing outdoors with "a girl in a tight sweater". I wonder what Manny could be nostalgic about.

— I think it's just another sign of his monomania. He'd probably heard this kind of music in Sweden when he was a child, latched on to it and never let go. Just like the maps. For all we know he listened to those same dozen records over and over and over, nothing else. That's his type. In a way it's a genius for living. Find what you like, stick to it.

— You really are bending over backwards to give this crazy old rich man the benefit of the doubt.

— I'm trying not to let my new life of crime spoil my humanity. I'm saying I felt a real warmth towards Manny that wasn't entirely wrapped up in greed. I watched him slide out the map, with that garish music blasting overhead, and I knew I was sitting across from a man who, if he wanted this thing, was going to pay whatever it took.

— So this warm feeling you experienced was, in fact, one entirely of greed, bubbling through your very pores.

— If you say so, Saddler. Anyway, out came the map. Up came the magnifying glass. I busied myself getting the documentation out of my briefcase. As with the cardinal, I had promised myself not to say a single word until the first impression was complete. In Manny's case, the first impression required me to listen to the whole jazz seventy-eight, to turn it over and listen to the other side, to select another record and listen to both sides of that. His concentration was phenomenal. Only his eyes moved, and very slowly. I'm still not sure what was going through his head. It did occur to me that Manny no doubt knew a hell of a lot more than I did about this piece, my research notwithstanding. Except that there wasn't a lot *to* know. In the map world pieces don't just fall out of the sky like this. Everyone knows everything. The vast majority of deals are made when someone finally decides to sell a whole raft of maps, and someone in, say, Shanghai will say, "Ah, at last, the one remaining fifteenth-century Yangtze," and negotiations commence. My map, though, was not only unknown, it was somehow almost *impossible*. It was a map, sure, but silver? In the thirteenth century? It was more like a piece of fine jewellery than a map. What to make of this? What purpose did it serve? For whom was it made? What was its history? How did it get stuffed in the back of an English atlas? I couldn't answer these questions. The thing is, there were no engraved maps in the period I'm talking about. Why would there be, when there wasn't even printing? The value in this piece lay in its mystery. I watched as Manny studied the map and hoped he didn't know either. There was a chance he'd say, "There are nine of these," or, one's constant fear, "This was made in Paris in 1928."

— You're not giving me a very positive impression of your confrères. The lonely cardinal, the agoraphobic Swede – are they all like that, your map people?

— Not to generalise, but . . . yes, they are. It's a type. Have you ever been to a stamp fair? Thick woolly jumpers in warm weather, yellow teeth, wild hair? It's not a sexy profession. Almost exclusively male. They make chess clubs look like tango classes. In the map world I think my colleagues were suspicious of me because I had decent hygiene and, by their standards, ultra-chic clothing. Don't get me wrong, I admired a lot of these people and I certainly never pitied them, but I was never going to fit in. Someone like Manny, though, is way over here on the scale. Imagine taking half an hour looking at my map and hardly blinking, much less pausing to say a word or two to me. He didn't even look up when I took a stroll along his cabinets, ogling his possessions. What nostalgia. There were pieces in there I'd been looking for, at least in the back of my mind, for fifteen years. Everybody had been looking for them.

— You didn't slip anything into your jacket pocket, did you?

— Ah, well, Manny's not one to let a map go missing, not for a second. He would be able to *smell* it if one of his pieces had been stared at too hard, never mind if it left his room. When he finally looked up he named the thin atlas I was looking at on the far side of the room, twenty feet away. "Nineteen sixty-four," he said. "Six thousand five hundred US." I whistled, to show him I was impressed: I knew the atlas was a Psolion and was worth ten times that sum today.

— Isn't it odd that he would mention money?

— Not at all. Dates, dollars, provenance – that's all he knows. Remember the full text of his letter to me, "Five pm, 16th." Doesn't exactly overdo the *politesse*.

— I suppose not.

— He beckoned me back over to his desk and motioned for me to pour us more berry wine. This may be because his hands trembled too badly for him to do so himself, but I'd noticed that he'd held the magnifying glass perfectly steady for all the time he'd spent inspecting every square millimetre of the Pilgrim Map.

— Is that what you called it?

— I'd started to. Has a nice, definitive ring to it, don't you think? *The* Pilgrim Map. As in, there is no other. Manny wasn't going to be influenced by that, though. He drank his tumbler of wine in one, then cracked back in his chair. I reckoned this was it, a yes or no on the spot. An offer or no offer, negotiation out of the question. Instead, Manny's face softened, he looked up at the ceiling, he gripped the armrests of his chair, and he began to narrate his life in maps, as if from a prepared and memorised text. It was fascinating – not the story, but the rote way he recounted forty-odd years of acquiring maps, building his wonderful, extremely private collection. Two hours, at least, without a pause. Where was Martha? When would he eat? He went, I swear, month by month through every purchase he had ever made – and very, very fast. I've no doubt he could have done the same trick alphabetically, or chronologically by date of map, or in ascending or descending order of value or appreciation or depreciation to the present day. It was a stunning feat.

— I can see why you say autistic.

— There you are. He paused only for two more tumblers of berry wine, which I'd suddenly grown fond of. To the extent that I could concentrate during such a long and detailed speech, I tried to fit my map into the litany of maps Manny listed. I was looking for a pattern in his acquisitions – there had to be a pattern, given what I'd surmised of the man's psychological make-up. As you know, if I'm an expert in anything it is Pacific maps from the period of the great voyages of discovery. Manny didn't own a single one. This was a good sign, because my map is European; a bad sign, because I'm weaker on the maps Manny ticked off down the years. I knew of perhaps one quarter, specifically, and a further third by hearsay. The pattern I was looking for at first was geographical. Perhaps he collected maps of only one region? Or perhaps he had started at one corner of Europe and moved relentlessly in one direction? Or perhaps he bought maps in another strict order, such as chronology? Or perhaps using an even more stubborn, autistic method having to do with numbers or the alphabet? If I could figure out what his list signified, I would have a better idea of how much or how little he would need to own the Pilgrim Map. I was convinced that he wouldn't buy the Pilgrim Map on its obvious, intrinsic merits as a work of art and of historical record. It had to fit into his scheme, which had probably lodged in his brain since he was a teenager. It had to be the missing piece of his own imagined puzzle. I was optimistic because when I'd written to him before our meeting about what the map roughly represented, he had agreed to see me – probably quite an effort for such a hermit. I reckoned he was going through his long list aloud not for my benefit, but for his own. He was visualising his puzzle, seeing if the new piece fitted.

— Did you manage to discern a pattern?

— After about one hour, I thought I had. Not surprisingly for such an eccentric man, Manny's yearning for maps seemed to have nothing to do with geography, nothing to do with history – and most importantly, little to do even with rarity.

— That was a strike against you.

— Certainly. For collectors, rarity is all. That's the rule. If there's only one of something, it is more valuable than if there are two. It doesn't really matter *what* it is. That's why the amateur stamp collector can get a private thrill out of a Penny Black, for what it is, what it represents. To a pro collector they're a dime a dozen. But find the only Penny Black ever personally affixed to a letter by Queen Victoria, even though it is physically the same stamp, and you're talking. What Manny's list was telling me, based on the half or so of it I could understand clearly, was that he had bought seemingly unrelated items, though each was unique. He obviously wouldn't tolerate even contemporaneous copies. But I assumed there had to be a thread. So I thought, rivers? Towns? Battles?

— Pilgrims?

— If only. I thought, Languages? Personages? Natural phenomena? It didn't take me too long to narrow it down. It wasn't physical. It wasn't historical. In a sense it was the most fundamental category you could think of.

— Don't make me guess.

— Well – and good for old Manny Horstedt, I say – it was map-making itself. It was technique, technology, science, engineering.

— Jackpot.

— Absolutely. His maps went all the way back. They'd skip a hundred or two hundred years until an advance was made. They lingered over the Greeks. He had one of every kind of map-making improvement in the three thousand years of the art – stopping, unsurprisingly, before images from space became the norm. Right there at the end of his fabulous collection, Saddler, he had a National Geographic map of the world from about 1957. The exact one I would have owned a few years later. But it was part of his collection right along with the Greeks and Mercator and every forgotten innovator in between. He'd spent all his life making the perfect collection of maps that would illustrate man's honing of his ability to document his physical surroundings to an increasingly accurate degree. It was a beautiful idea, and he'd done it all himself. He'd made a museum exhibit that could last forever. It made me want to cry. Not a collection for connoisseurs to ooh and aah over because they were so rare and so valuable – though many of them, as I've said, were incredibly so – but a plain linear record. You can find this sort of thing in books, hundreds of them, but Manny had the genuine articles. Every single one definitely the work of the original maker.

— And what you were showing him used a technique you'd never seen before, from a time when it wasn't even supposed to exist?

— With anyone but Manny I would have tried to make my map mystical, even occult. Manny wasn't the sort to fall for that. I'd have to sell him on the map's physical merits. I couldn't wait to hear what he would say when he'd finished with his hours-long list. When I realised the dates of his acquisitions were approaching the present day, I perked up. "Now this," Manny said, as if he'd bought my map already. I said I had brought along the documentation of my research, and I started to reach for my briefcase. He put up a hand and said, "No. I am tired." He had a rusty old robot's voice. "I will contact you."

— After making you sit there for hours? Nothing?

— Nothing.

— Not even an idea of what he was thinking?

— I don't take him for a dirty dealer. He would have told me if he knew how the map was made. He didn't want to appear ignorant, so he's going to take some time, do some studying, find what he finds. The good news is that he was intrigued enough to take the time. You should really *see* this map, Saddler. I was tempted to bring it along. You've never seen anything like it.

— I like the idea of your progress, Hart. Go for the religious and mystical angle with the Church, go for the technical side with the crazy collector. I suppose selling it as a work of art will be next.

— Clever you. Yes. So far no one will even talk to me. Such snobs. Such know-it-alls. I'll find an art man eventually. Meanwhile my hopes rest on Manny. I got a great feeling about him, as if there really were a slot in one of his cabinets exactly the width of my map. I left there in a good mood. This quickly changed.

— What happened?

— It hadn't quite stopped raining. It was very dark outside – I'd been with Manny for about three hours. As soon as I'd said goodbye to his wife, closed the gate behind me and turned right on the pavement, I saw the shape of a man walking towards me about thirty or forty yards away. There were street lamps, but he was walking in the shadows between two of them and was dressed in a hat and dark suit. The moment he looked up from under the brim of his hat and saw me, he turned quickly and picked up his pace in the opposite direction.

— Did you see what he looked like?

— In the dark, from that distance, no – even though because I'd had some experience being followed I very consciously memorised what I could see. This wasn't much. He was tall and thin, his gait was that of a fit but probably middle-aged man, and his clothes – don't ask me how I know this from a distance –

looked well cut. The soles of his shoes rang out on the pavement, in a hollow-wooden way, which makes me think they were bespoke.

— A rich, fit man, following you. Was this the same man you'd seen before?

— Very probably.

— Honest to God, Hart, can't you at least get to the bottom of that? How long's it been? You talk about your map, your crime, but if someone's following you . . . I think it must be Cambon.

— Too tall.

— No, I mean your good friend Cambon probably sent someone. I'm imagining a detective as obsessed about solving crimes as your Manny is about missing map links. I'm thinking Cambon won't sleep, et cetera, until he has his man. Isn't that how these terriers work? And as far as you've told me, you're his only suspect. He must be having you watched – you, the paedophile necrophilliac. He'd be crazy not to. Or, in case you haven't thought of this, it could be the girl's father. Hart, these people *want* you. You're being watched. It could be all of them. It could be Stenniman. Why can't you see this? You're skating over everything and taking a terrible risk.

— I've spoken to Cambon in the past week.

— He contacted you?

— No. I rang him up from my usual chair in Green Park. And you're right: I remain his only suspect. I always make such a mess of my conversations with Cambon. I say, "I still feel so guilty," which is true, but he says, "Oh? Do you want to say more?" Then I'll say, "I don't feel guilty about murdering Annette." And he says, "Don't you?" And I have to say, "No, I mean I don't feel guilty about murdering her, I feel guilty about my lust."

— Why don't you use the word "embarrassed" instead of "guilty"?

— There's an idea. But the damage was done during his first interrogation with me, when I must have seemed almost to be bragging about getting away with murder. That's how completely stupid I am. I think Cambon wants to charge me.

— Come on. With murder?

— Probably not. Or not yet. I think he wants to get the crime back in the news, and one way to do that is to charge me, with something. I'd bet on indecent exposure.

— It was more than a year ago. Why would he have waited? Wouldn't Cambon look like an idiot?

— No, he'd look like someone who thinks he knows who committed the vile quasi-sexual murder of a child, but who can't yet prove it, and who is putting the screws on the man he thinks did the deed.

— I hope you're wrong about that. I mean, if you're charged and it turns out you never even told your own wife . . .

— It has occurred to me that such an omission would not put me a good light. In those circumstances I would have to say that I didn't tell Mary because she was in a fragile state.

— Oh, you'd put it all on her?

— Well, it's partly true, you know. When's the last time you saw Mary?

— Three, four years ago.

— You'd find her changed.

— That's only to be expected. I daresay you've changed, too.

— Well, what do you remember about Mary in the old days? When did you first meet her?

— I remember exactly. It was four months before you were married. I met her at that Italian restaurant. We had a good time.

— Tell me, honestly, what you thought of her.

— Hah. Other than that she was taking you away from me?

— Cut it out, Saddler. What did you make of Mary?

— What everyone else did. You're crazy, Hart. Mary and I are friends, for heaven's sake. She was the highest-quality girl in the room, OK? I thought she transcended her more frivolous circle. And if I may say so, I think you rose in her estimation when she found out your oldest friend was gay. She wanted to go shopping with me, for example. We talked about books. I think I may have done you some favours there. But come on, she was vivacious and interested in life and utterly in love with you.

— Nice to hear.

— And the way you describe her now, I think you're talking about simple depression.

— What's simple about that? And why is it depression if I'm causing the whole thing?

— Look here. I don't have *that* many close married friends anymore. But without exception this phase in their lives is rotten with exactly what you describe, or most of the elements. Except that, I might add, you're rather piling on with the extracurriculars.

— But that can't be the cause of her problems if she doesn't know what I'm up to. Unless, of course, she *does* know, and she's put a detective on my tail.

— You've said even your little daughters can gauge the mood. Don't you think Mary can, as well?

— What if she's only pretending? It's a nasty thought, I know, but what if Mary's being miserable and having me followed and blackmailed just to drag me down? Or out of revenge, because I've made such a mess of my business?

— I don't think she can pretend to have an eating disorder. And Hart? I've never been one to give anyone advice, and I hesitate to start now, but in a second I'm not only going to advise you, I'm going to *beg* you to stop seeing this girlfriend of yours.

— I'm due at her place in an hour.

— Please. Don't go. Just stop.

— No can do, Saddler. I won't let you interrupt my flow. I'm not going to be some monochrome *organism* any longer. And on a side note, if you make me read one more book about evolutionary biology, I'll kill myself. I want free will.

— You're not telling this woman anything, are you? She might be a plant. I'm not saying you don't have your animal attraction, but it doesn't sound . . . plausible. I mean, that she'd single you out of a crowd.

— Thanks a lot.

— You know what I mean. It isn't *usual*.

— All the more reason to take advantage.

— You're impossible.

— Maybe. You'll have to humour your old friend.

— What would your brother say?

— Colin? He's not my conscience. He's the conscience of the world. And anyway, if he's not sewing up some thirteen-year-old girl's fistula right now, he's screwing a pair of Danish nurses. He doesn't have time to condemn common adultery. Why are you looking at me that way?

— I won't lecture you. I don't even want to judge. But I'm out on a limb with you on the map project, and I'm trying to absorb some of your other troubles. I'll help where I can. I really will. Still, you predicate most of this on wanting to save your family – that is, when you're not exerting your *freedom*, right?

— More or less, Saddler. Why so serious?

— Because I don't buy the girlfriend part. I'll only say it once more: put an end to Sophie.

— Or else what?

— Or else nothing, from me. I'm saying if it blows up there's no point to any of this. What are you getting out of her, really? It sounds cold, humourless.

— Look who's talking, Saddler. It's sex. It's manhood. What else can I tell you? In a few minutes I'll make my way over there. She's never missed a date. She'll be in the middle of getting ready for whatever her evening holds. I'll simply *take* her, right there on the floor if necessary. Few words will be said. Think of what you've been up to for a quarter of a century, Saddler, and tell me I'm wrong to have discovered this form of entertainment. Beats sitting around at home being told I'm no use. Argue with that, Saddler.

— I don't have the breath.

— Exactly. And I won't fight with you. You just have to trust me. She's not a plant. She never asks me anything except to fuck her. God, listen to me – I'm using the language.

— And where will Mary think you are?

— She knows I'm seeing you. She'll expect me after dinner.

— Do you expect me to cover for you?

— If you'd be so kind. I was going to bring that up.

— I'm leaving. I have to go.

— Come on, don't be angry, Saddler. Just turn off your phone. That's what I do.

— I'm leaving.

— Hey, don't go away in that mood. I'm sorry, Saddler.

— Forget all that. Ring me when you have news. Think about what I said. Be careful. Here's thirty for the bill.

*London, late that same night*

Darius Saddler is asleep in bed. His telephone rings and he has to walk into the small living room to answer.

— Saddler, it's me. I need your help.

— Mmm . . . What time is it? What's going on? Where are you?

— Sorry to wake you. It's three in the morning. Are you alone?

— Am I alone? Let me see . . . Yes, I'm alone. What's going on?

— Something happened.

— Are you all right? Do you need me to come and get you?

— That won't be necessary. I'm right outside.

— Outside what, Hart?

— Your flat. Funny I've never been here before. You're on the first floor, correct? If you go to your window you will see me across the street, loitering . . . Ah, there you are. I'm the one meekly waving.

— I'll be right down.

— . . .

— I *love* what you've done with the place, Saddler. I'll just sit on this paint can.

— We can go in there – it's the *breakfast nook.*

— Lovely. Would you call this "battleship grey"?

— Would you like a cup of coffee? Are you very drunk?

— Yes, please. And no drunker than you are, as not a drop has passed my lips since you left me in a fit of pique some ten hours ago.

— Is that why you're here? I wasn't angry, Hart, just frustrated and a little annoyed by your stubbornness. I'm sorry if that distressed you. If you move about two feet to your right I can get at the coffee.

— You know, one thing I was sure about: you are the sort of man who will have a dressing gown handy at all hours, and here you are wearing one. You might have been expecting me. And you're also the sort of chap who'd have a dram of brandy right above the sink, there, to add to the coffee of uninvited guests. I suggest you join me.

— Sure, fine. Look, I said I was sorry. I didn't mean to—

— No. No no no. I would have thought nothing more of your hectoring, your patronising tone, the nerve of your telling me how to conduct my affairs. No. It isn't that. That's not why I'm here. I've not been idle since we parted. In fact, for the first half-hour of my walk in the direction of Sophie's house, I gave serious thought to taking your advice, hopping on the Tube and going home. I would place at five thirty, post meridian, the moment when I said to myself, "To hell with Saddler," and continued on my intended way.

— Here's the coffee. I'll let you pour the brandy.

— Thank you, and I will.

— Are you all right?

— Far from it. Cheers. And you will indulge my narrative.

— Go on, then.

— I have to say you've been dismissive of my soulless affair with Sophie. You didn't understand the upside. Rather hypocritically, you claimed not to see what I could gain from a purely sexual relationship. Well, let me tell you, during that *next* half-hour, as I zeroed in on her flat – *that's* what I get out of it. The anticipation. If you're not familiar with that sensation, I'm . . .

— Yes?

— I'm Noël Coward.

— Got you.

— I never had a French girlfriend, you know. It felt as if fate had given me another chance. I could go back to being twenty-five years old and having a French girlfriend. It's something I had missed. I was making up for that oversight. Except for the going out to the café and tossing our heads in laughter over oysters and white wine, it was exactly as I'd always fantasised. Sophie lives in a basement flat in Bayswater. Rented. I don't dare ask how she can afford that, but one assumes her company pays. She doesn't say much about work, but she seems awfully busy. I suppose she hopes to be some sort of producer of documentaries one day. In the meantime she's a film-stock mule.

— You haven't described her.

— Yes, I have. She looks like Annette, ten years older. Her only flaw is cigarette smoking. Otherwise she is fresh as spring flowers. Also, she simply *inflames* me. By the time I get to the steps down to her door my pulse is racing, I have the virility of a thousand men, I am validated as a male.

— Good for you. This would be by way of an excuse?

— Naturally. I am blaming an insurmountable human instinct for the catastrophe that may be about to befall my family.

— May be?

— I'll tell you. She heard my steps on the stairs and opened the door before I knocked. All was as usual. She wore a dressing gown, her hair was wet from showering, she kissed me and said we didn't have much time. She keeps a tidy place. We fell onto the bed. She was laughing, and I asked her why. She said she was laughing because she was happy to see that I was as eager as she was, and in a hurry. Isn't that wonderful?

— I suppose so.

— The tearing at my clothes must have taken half a minute, the parting of her robe a second more. One had only reached the delicate kissing of her neck before the telephone rang.

— How deflating.

— This had happened before, but never before had she answered. She apologised, she didn't let go of me, but she picked up. She said hello in English. She listened, she didn't say more, she turned off the phone. Then she pushed away from me. I asked if there was something wrong. She said, "It was for you."

— . . . ?

— All right, here's what she said next. She said, "A man just told me, 'You can tell Mr Hart that Porter rang. Tell him that. Tell him Porter rang.' Who is Porter?" Now what could I say? That I knew someone named Porter and had given him her number? So I asked her, "What did he sound like?" She thought for a moment and said, "American."

— Your man of a thousand voices.

— I told Sophie not to worry, that it was someone from work. That was a stupid thing to say. She wanted to know how this Porter had got her number, if it hadn't been from me. I asked if her number happened to be listed. She said that it was, through her company but not in her name. What could I tell her? I'm still holding her in my arms, but she's pushing back, frightened. I said I'd given no one her number. I promised. I asked her why the hell I would do that. I suppose I must have been . . . holding her down, because she scratched at my face – she missed, thank God, but she got me here – look, below my ear. She was really scared. I rolled away and she got off the bed. She demanded to know what was going on. I told myself, "Think,

think." I began to speak. I said, "Come here; it's all right. I'll tell you the truth."

— You didn't.

— Of course not. I told her that the person who calls himself Porter is, in fact, an older man, rather pathetic, from work, who followed me to her flat a few weeks ago. He gets a kick out of this. He's not dangerous. He has a million secrets of his own. We're not in any kind of trouble. I pointed out to Sophie that I'm really the only one who *could* get into trouble. I eased her back on to the bed and comforted her.

— How smooth you are.

— Yes, and I comforted the *hell* out of her for half an hour and all seemed to be well where she's concerned.

— This leaves you with the fact the Porter has even more goods on you.

— I don't know. Can Porter really follow every single one of the people he's running? And why would he single me out for a paltry six-fifty every now and then?

— You said five hundred.

— I made a mistake.

— Maybe Porter is many people, a ring. That would explain all the accents.

— Could be. But more likely it's Mary who's smelled a rat, had me followed and is now starting to turn the screws.

— What I don't understand is why you came here. Where does poor Mary think you are?

— I didn't come here. I went straight home. Saddler, I spent from seven until midnight being the perfect husband and father. I dined *en famille*. I tucked up my girls. I invented a bedtime story about acrobats from the former Yugoslavia whose star girl trapeze artist is saved from a fatal fall by the trunk of an Indian elephant. I chatted with Mary about you and other matters. It was only after midnight that I said to "poor Mary" that I had to get out of the house for a long think.

— What did you tell her you were going to think long about?

— Business. I was full of false optimism as I went out the door. That was, what, three or four hours ago?

— And you walked all the way here?

— Looking over my shoulder the whole time. I wasn't followed.

— One would expect Porter to raise his price, after this.

— Which is why I'm going to call his bluff.

— And when you get home at dawn, stinking of brandy?

— She might expect that, as you and I seem to have been seeing more of each other than usual lately.

— Sensible, because you know I'll stick to whatever story you want to tell.

— Thank you.

— I really will, you know. I'll do what you want.

— Great friends expect no less from each other. One day I will return the favour.

— So that's it. Do you have the taxi fare? Want me to call one?

— I'd rather . . . I'd rather just stay for a little longer, Saddler. I wish I could see things more clearly. I don't want things to get on *top* of me. You know, I was reading about a map thief in Canada. He stole a number of maps over a period of time. Not even to sell. Just for his own pleasure. Poor man, it was like pornography to him. Like my collectors, he *needed* to own these things. To look at in secret. He wasn't in the business. He was like Mad Manny without the funds. So he stole a few precious maps, and he was caught. Do you know what they did to him?

— The Canadians?

— Yes. They imprisoned him for four years. Doesn't that seem harsh? He didn't even hurt the maps – far from it. The maps were safer with him than they'd been in the libraries. And at least someone was enjoying them.

— Are you worried about going to prison? For one map?

— You say "one map". But the total haul of the Canadian was worth about a tenth of the price of this "one map" – if I'm at all right about what it's worth. If we continue to call it just a map, then it's one of the most valuable of all time.

— So it's more a work of art. That doesn't change anything. It's still grand larceny.

— Well, there's another case, in America this time. A man who is arguably he most successful map dealer in the world. For three decades he's led the field. I've sold him maps in my time, so has Rory. And he was caught red-handed – he dropped a razor on a library floor after he'd been conducting "research", the librarian became suspicious, called security, had him searched, and his briefcase contained half a dozen maps he'd sliced out of the books he'd supposedly been studying. Since then up to a hundred maps he's dealt have proved to be stolen. And a custodial sentence is a certainty. He might get ten years in prison.

— So stop. Destroy the thing. Forget all about it.

— Do you know one of the many reasons why I don't mind if I go down, Saddler?

— What is that?

— Do you ever lie awake at night wondering why you do what you do?

— In what sense?

— In the sense of your overall motivation.

— I suppose I do. I've never come to any conclusions.

— I'll tell you mine, then. If I go down, if I'm taken away, if everything is blown, what will people think?

— People?

— You know, *people*. Mary's friends. They'll say, "Well I'll be *damned*," is what they'll say. "A fraud? An adulterer? Wanted for indecency or murder in France? Henry? He's *done* it." In this way I win the respect of society. And that, Saddler, is what it would appear to be all about.

— Respect?

— Prestige. It is all prestige. Human beings do everything they do for status. I'm sure you've noticed. Everything, including sex, follows from prestige. There is no other way to account for behaviour. However unconscious this may be, it is observable truth. And it is why, at this stage, I can't stop myself from going ahead with the plan which, if it works, makes me somewhat rich; and if it fails, gives me the prestige of the outlaw. I'd hold my head high on the way to the cells.

— You're coming over all Camus.

— Take my parents. What do they do? My mother organises for the Conservative Party. This takes very little of her time, but in her small, vicious circle it gives her prestige. My father, on the other hand, has turned inward. His main hobby has long been time-lapse photography of plants and flowers. His latest project is an avocado. He planted the stone, set up his camera, and for two and a half years he has photographed the avocado exactly eight times every day. He wakes up in the middle of the night to clack the shutter.

— How does this gain him prestige?

— It sends the message that he is a solid enough man to turn his back on society and live in the pure realm of his choosing – in this case, the documentation of the life of an avocado. It says he eschews the social and material fruits of a long career in favour of an inner existence. It says he disdains the pedestrian activities of his wife. It says no amount of material wealth would change the way he lives his days – that the millionaire is pissing in the wind. If others were to say or think that what he did was boring, his refutation is in the pleasure he claims to take in the act of avocado-watching itself. There are plenty of avenues open to the man who might otherwise consider himself to be a failure – to a man like me, for example. There's always Buddhism. Instead of having to say, "I didn't make it as an investment banker," you can say you chose Buddhism. The prestige lies in the suspicion successful bankers have that the Buddhist might be getting more out of life.

— So instead of Buddhism, you've chosen a life of crime.

— You can't "choose". You can *say* you chose. The implication is that you have deliberately followed a higher path. But you didn't. When you fall from grace, you land where fate deposits you, and you make what you can of your new whereabouts.

— I'm glad you've intellectualised the whole thing. And at least now I know you're not doing this on purpose, that you're being swept along by unconscious forces.

— It's true. And it's possible to know of this process and to be its victim, both at the same time.

— Don't you think you're drinking too much?

— No doubt. I believe it helps with cementing the moral conviction.

— I'm afraid I have to disagree with your analysis.

— Good luck. My argument is impermeable.

— A lot of people, I've noticed, are looking for love. Unconsciously or not.

— Oh, *that*.

— Don't you think?

— I'm probably too repressed to get into the area of love. Perhaps you're not. But it does strike me that some people – I'm not necessarily pointing fingers here – get what they need out of the search for love. They're in love with the concept of love, not with its object.

— How very profound. How grown-up you've become.

— Try to be nice. In any case it's easier for you to entertain lofty ideas of love and so on, when some of us have practical problems to solve.

— You're speaking of the blackmail again.

— Yes. The *extortion*. And here is my considered decision: I'm going to meet Porter halfway. I'm also going to trap him into dropping a clue that Mary's behind the whole scheme. I'll give him the Annette blackmail, but I won't give him the Sophie blackmail. The Sophie blackmail I simply won't pay. My family can survive a casual affair. Mary can survive it, especially as it's likely she's orchestrated the whole thing. She'll have had her revenge, such as it is. I'll tell Porter so, next time he's in touch. On the other hand, the Annette blackmail I'll have to continue to pay. If that story's blown I'll end up on some register of sex offenders. As I've said, that's the climate these days. It would be like the ostracism you've complained of, only ten times worse. My theory is that if I agree to keep paying the Annette blackmail, it won't be worth Porter's time to bust me on the Sophie affair.

— You make me laugh, Hart. You really do. You're hilarious. That's really your decision? To negotiate with a blackmailer?

— Yes.

— God help you, then.

— Thanks. And furthermore, just to get this thing *over* with, I'm seeing an art man in the morning.

— It is the morning.

— Ah, well, would you have a spare razor and a toothbrush?

— Of course.

— Before I beautify myself, there's a little something I want to show you. It's in my briefcase by the door.

— Don't get up. I'll fetch the case . . . Here we are. Let me guess – a stack of notes, as a down payment on my cooperation?

— Not quite, Saddler. I've brought you the map.

— What? You walked across London in the middle of the night with that thing in your briefcase?

— Happily. What a pleasure to be mugged for my phone, while carrying *this* around. Have a look.

— Holy . . .

— . . . ?

— Jesus.

— I thought you'd say that. I wanted your approval. Have a look with the magnifying glass. Here.

— This is . . . This is *eerie*.

— To your untrained eye, it is eerie. To my trained one, it is a bloody miracle.

— This . . . this *object*, is eight hundred years old?

— Give or take.

— But I mean – you'd need an electron microscope to make out the trails. Are those *flowers*?

— And I have absolutely no fucking idea how it was made. Again, the only analogy I've got is the silicon chip.

— Well, then, you've got to ask someone. Swear them to secrecy.

— You're starting to see our problem. Selling this map – if we must still call it a map – is a bit like fencing a Rembrandt: too important to get away with. Except in a way it's the opposite, because no one knows this thing exists. If the Vatican buys it, they'll do so knowing it's of dubious ownership. We rely on their stealth and their discretion and their understanding of venial sin. If Manny buys it – an outcome devoutly to be wished – he's the sort to take the secret to his grave. I assume both Cardinal Shumm and Mad Manny are perfectly aware that they're looking at dodgy goods. In a few hours, the art man will know it, too. So I've come to another decision. From now on, because you've been kind enough to agree to help me, this is Nathan's map. He found it in Europe during the war, when he was "something to do with refugees"; the story goes that he bought it fair and square from a Jewish family he helped to settle in London, whose name he never told anyone. He left all of his belongings to your parents, who left this map specifically to you, Nathan's favourite, not knowing its value. I want to be upfront about this story, Saddler. It's what I'll tell the art man. It's what you'll tell your sisters. It's the one big lie, and we have to stick to it right to the end.

— It's . . . beautiful.

— Isn't it? I knew you'd think so. And to think, Saddler, you own a tenth of it.

— Make it a third, and I'll say anything you want.

— I knew I could count on you, you bastard. A third it is. Well done with the negotiating. You're going to see a lot of money out of this. You can tear down those stables, dig a better pool.

— Is there something wrong with my pool?

— Sorry. Of course not. You can plant cacti, or whatever grows down there these days.

— Who's your art man?

— His name is Xavier "So-So" Lobke. "So-So" because that's what he calls practically every work of art that comes under his nose. He's also sometimes called the "X-Man", because of his first initial and the spooky, negative connotations of the letter X. I've never met him. Naturally he's – sorry, Saddler – gay as the 1890s.

— I'm trying to imagine a queer named Xavier Lobke who *doesn't* turn out to be an art dealer. What nationality?

— English father via the Ukraine, long dead. Belgianish mother, perhaps aristocratic, who still lives. Xavier himself is about sixty years old.

— Why Xavier?

— Because he carries around a grudge the size of Greenland and he's crooked. His dream was always to buy and sell, hold on to great works on the side, then retire at about forty to Cap Louise and set himself up in a villa to entertain great wits and beautiful young men.

— He wouldn't have been the first.

— You're thinking of Berenson. But no. It didn't work out for him. Some say he didn't have the touch, or even the taste. Some say he took too many risks. Some say he was too greedy, others that he was too generous. It didn't help that at around the time he turned forty – the watershed, his target for freedom – half of his closest friends and his great love all died.

— That would have been at the beginning of the Dark Time.

— Which you know only too well. Thank you for not dying, by the way.

— You're welcome.

— Xavier is so annoyed that his life didn't work out as planned that for the last twenty years he's gone ever-so-slightly bent.

— Sounds familiar.

— He's never been charged with anything, but his lifestyle has improved immeasurably in recent times without any visible deals to back up such a change. Let's just say he's got his villa. Not a sprawling one, but impressive enough to represent at least three or four secret sales, and big ones.

— What's his area?

— The big time: bloody Impressionists. They *never* go away, those guys. And there's always some flaky rich man who wants one to himself, just to gaze at in his airy study and perhaps to show to a handful of friends who are sworn to keep mum. I don't get it, myself, and frankly Cezanne can go to hell for all I care, but the secret buyer is the criminal's friend. Do you remember George Burling? Rich tosser banker who used to orbit my group about ten years ago?

— Sure. Napoleon complex, pint-sized alcoholic, hair plugs, user of hookers – sorry, escorts – arch, rather brilliant.

— George bought stuff from So-So Lobke. It's easy to say that people who buy Impressionists have no taste, but my view is, whatever makes them happy. George once took me aside at one of his parties and dragged me into the "gallery" he'd built for himself in his actually rather wonderful flat in Chelsea. He only vaguely knew me, but he knew what I did for a living and I think he wanted someone in the know to be flabbergasted by his collection. The cocaine and booze made him lecture me at length, at volume, about the exactly four paintings he owned. He said practically outright that they were stolen goods. "You don't even know what you're looking at!" he shouted, when I failed to faint in the presence of his Pissarro. I tried to say all the right things, to reassure good old George, but I was thinking a) what I was looking at was an example of the worst sort of nostalgic, Christmas-present-wrapping *nothing* and b) it was a forgery.

— How could you tell? It's not your field.

— Because the original, which used to be in the Jeu de

Paume, was considered so inferior that it's now across the river in the basement of the Musée d'Orsay. Even the original didn't make the cut. Dear, oblivious little George paid a million three for his bad copy.

— He told you he paid that much?

— Of course he did. What's the point, otherwise? The painting represents his success – his *prestige*. The others were probably originals, I think.

— Well, good for George. Three out of four. That's probably a better strike rate than most museums.

— Yes, but so dispiriting to stand in a windowless white room looking at a dull painting of a snowy lane, or the *stupid* Mont Sainte-Victoire.

— You're contradicting yourself, Hart. You're supposed to see these things from the owner's point of view. If it gives him pleasure, so what?

— I suppose you're right, and that is my position. But for what those lousy paintings cost . . . Can't think that way. It's George's money. I suppose I feel sorry for him. At least the stolen goods we're selling are real.

— Let's hope so.

— And Lobke might be our man. Obviously, he'd be buying for someone else, so we'll take a hit on the price. But he knows the George Burlings of this world, the people who want to own something because it's irrationally expensive. It must give them a great rush to hand over a million pounds for a sweaty canvas they're not supposed to show to anyone.

— Could it be that they sincerely love art?

— Try to imagine George Burling, all alone – he's never married, you know – standing in his gallery looking at the fake Pissarro for the millionth time. I find that depressing. I know about you and music, for example, and I understand completely. Doesn't cost you anything to sit alone in your chateau listening to Buxtehude—

— Buxtehude?

— Or whatever flavour you fancy. And music can't be fake. You can be all alone and cry or be spiritually elevated, this I comprehend. To me a painting is decoration, something to break up a wall.

— Do you think George Burling might want your map?

— That would surprise me. He wants things that are immediately known to his social acquaintances, so that he doesn't have to say, "I paid more than a million for this map, you know," and then have to explain why it's so valuable. I don't know why men like George don't just have piles of gold ingots lying about the place, if they only mean to emphasise their wealth. Besides, gold ingots would be more beautiful to look at than any Cezanne. Anyway, if not George, someone *like* George.

— What time do you meet Lobke?

— Not until ten o'clock. It's going to be a long day. I'm going to try to arrange seeing Sophie in the afternoon. Would you mind if I just curled up in a corner and went to sleep?

— Use the bed, Hart. I've had plenty of rest. I'll wake you at eight. We'll get you that toothbrush and razor. I'll find you a pressed shirt. OK?

— You're very kind.

— Oh, and Hart?

— Yes?

— While you're sleeping, do you mind if I stay with the map?

*Later that day, at the Pigeon in Kentish Town*

— It's safe to say I have news, Saddler.

— Take off your coat and have a seat first.

— I know I look a mess. Took ages to find a taxi in this rain.

— Taxi? Hey, big spender. It must be good news, then.

— Pardon me while I take a few deep breaths. Ah, there. Yes, it's good news. And then it's not. So much has happened. I hope you have time.

— What else would I be doing?

— If I haven't lost track of a whole day, I left your flat at eight-thirty this morning.

— With grim determination, map in hand.

— I cleared my head with a brisk walk to Marble Arch. The potential big spender in me taxied all the way to Lobke's house in – who would have guessed? – Belsize Park. I could tell the journey was going to take an hour. I might be late. I thought of calling ahead, but then my phone began to ring. First on the line was Father Anthony – remember him?

— *Do* I.

— He said he had an important message from "him", meaning Cardinal Schumm, who was in Thailand on Church business.

— Ho ho. Do you think cardinals wear undies beneath their cassocks?

— A first good sign was that Father Anthony only identified himself and the cardinal by implication, and didn't want to speak at length on my mobile phone. This suggested guile and therefore fraud – very auspicious. He was willing to say that the two experts of the cardinal's choosing were ready to inspect "it", here in London, at the end of the week. Perhaps incautiously, he also said that "he", meaning Cardinal Schumm again, was "fascinated" by "it". Father Anthony said, "this is rare", meaning not the map but the cardinal's fascination. Or both. I said that I was delighted, and that I awaited a meeting place and time. I said "it" would be with me. He signed off with the hope that next time I was in Rome . . .

— He remembered your hair.

— Presumably. By this time the driver was looking at me in the mirror, assuming I was a drug mule or a Swiss banker. When the next call came in I closed the partition.

— Mad Manny?

— Manny's wife. We had almost the exact same conversation, minus the Thailand reference. Manny was "fascinated" and wanted to take another look at "it" at the end of the week. She was able to give me a set time on Friday, back at Manny's house.

— This is fantastic news. You've done it perfectly, then. They're playing the game.

— So it would seem. Without revealing anything specific on the phone to either of them, though, I was able to convey the idea that I'd spoken to others and an electric climate of *auction* was in the air.

— You insist on pushing this to the limit, don't you?

— That's the point. Next up was Sophie, who was worried about the Porter phone call. By then my spirits were so revived that I told her I'd sorted it out, Porter was indeed a lunatic from the office, but that he meant no harm. I stuck to my original story. She said she needed me, needed me badly. I said I might be able to see her later on in the day, which was what I'd wanted to do anyway.

— I'm assuming you spent the whole ride looking out of the back window of the taxi, making sure you weren't followed.

— I did a bit of that. Not to worry. I simply agreed to meet Sophie at the unusual hour of three thirty, which would allow me to celebrate with her – though she wouldn't necessarily have to know I was celebrating – and to get home to the family at a reasonable supposed work-day hour.

— I don't like that part.

— Next call, throat-tighteningly enough, was from Mary. I told her I'd stayed at your flat because I'd walked and walked while having my long think, and it was closer to the office. She said she'd rung you, and you'd confirmed this.

— True enough.

— Thank you.

— You were having an excellent morning.

— Yes. And then Porter rang.

— You're so *popular*. I'm lucky if my phone rings once every other day.

— I did what I told you I would do. I told Porter I'd meet him halfway on the blackmail. He spoke with a German accent, this time. I'm sure Porter's only one man, though. He laughed at me. He said I was being "cute". I stood my ground. I said I assumed he'd reached similar impasses during his extortionist career, where "little men" like me have had enough. I said if he pushed me I'd cancel the whole deal and take my medicine even on the Annette front. To my surprise, he agreed. We're stuck at six fifty roughly every ten days.

— That's more than twenty grand a year, Hart.

— Let's just pretend I have an older child at school. Other people cope with that sort of thing. When I get the money for the map, I'll negotiate a lump-sum deal with Porter to bring the whole thing to an end.

— Blackmailers never stop.

— I'll make it worth his while to tell me who he is, so we're even.

— Good luck with that.

— I was now pulling up to Lobke's house. I was expecting him, at that hour, to greet me at the door in a velvet robe, blurry eyed, perhaps a glass of morning champagne in his hand, a taut-buttocked, half-naked youth peeking out at me from the kitchen.

— Instead he was fully dressed, sober, alone and businesslike?

— No. He was precisely as I'd expected, including the half-naked youth. It's wonderful how often people run to type. Is that the life to which you aspire, Saddler?

— Not . . . specifically.

— He's very well preserved, So-So Lobke. A great head of salt-and-pepper hair. A reckless glint in his eye. I agreed that a glass of champagne would be a good idea, so he conveyed the order to his young sex slave and we repaired to the conservatory. It was jungle-hot in there so that he could grow bananas and other phallic plants. His sex slave brought us a chilled bottle and a second glass. Then Lobke began to talk to me as if we were picking up from a previous conversation. So far I'd only said, "Hello," and "Yes, please," and off he launched into a gossipy story about a woman friend of his who had recently driven a car over her husband, four times. "Wasn't even *slightly* injured," he said, shaking his head. There was no point to this story, nor to the next three or four stories he wanted to tell me.

— Pissed?

— I don't think so. Just convivial. And I guess he was trying to figure out if I wanted to have sex with him.

— Strapping young fellow like you, with tinted hair? No doubt about it.

— Well. He was all charm. He got round to asking me how I'd heard of him. I said he wasn't unknown, and I mentioned George Burling. He smiled fondly at the name, perhaps remembering the shitty forgery he'd sold George for a million three. I stopped myself from saying that I'd seen the "Pissarro" and winking. I didn't want Lobke to think I was trading in fakes. He asked if I'd like a mushroom omelette, as only his sex slave could make them. He told more stories while our breakfast was prepared. Finally, while we were eating, he asked about me. I gave him a rough outline of my career and the story, mentioning you but not by name, of how a wonderful object had come into my possession. I made it more obvious to him than I had with the others that my map was not technically mine to sell, but that I wanted to sell it anyway.

— Did you tell him about the cardinal and Manny?

— I mentioned "other interest", but I didn't want to put him off. I hope I was able to make it plain that I could sell the map at a good price elsewhere, but that elsewhere was more risky. "How much are we talking about?" he asked me, without yet having seen the map. This took me by surprise, but I managed to say, "I think I'll let you be the judge of that." Sometimes I say,

"Whatever's fair." I hate to be the one to name a figure, based on the superstition that my buyer will look up from the map and name an astronomical sum that had never occurred to me even in dreams. He kept talking, and still he didn't ask to see the map. He told me about the "old days", by which I think he meant the 70s and early 80s, when "times were tight" and "awfully sad, really". Then he perked up and said, "I like you, and I think we're going to do business."

— Without seeing the map.

— That's right. He became so straightforward I thought it must be some sort of trick. He said, "I'll have Arthur clear away breakfast, and then I'll look at what you've brought, and then I will make you an offer. Is that fine with you?" I said it was. He said he would take my word for what the object *was*, but that he would be the one to name a price. There would be a little negotiation, he said, but "not much". He said, "I don't hold on to things. If a buyer doesn't come immediately to mind, I won't be interested. I will want to sell this on in a week to ten days." I said I understood. He said, "Whatever the agreed price, I will pay you half right away – I mean today – and half when I sell it on."

— Rum.

— That's what I said. I said his terms were unacceptable to me. I said that was not a way I could do business in this case. Can you believe this? We were arguing terms before he'd even seen the map in question. Arthur the sex slave came in to—

— Please stop calling him that.

— Sorry. Arthur the *manservant* came in to clear away our plates. I revealed the map and handed it over with my magnifying glass. "Tell me, tell me," Lobke said. So I told him what I thought the map was. What I *knew* the map was.

— Excuse me just a second, Hart. Don't want to interrupt. I mentioned a while ago, regarding your new hair, that I was brought up not to make personal remarks. I'll make an exception. Your hands are trembling. No, they're shaking. What's up?

— Just let me get through this. Believe me, I'll get to what happened. It isn't nice. And it isn't the drink, if that's what you're implying. Speaking of which.

— . . .

— Cheers, Saddler.

— Cheers.

— The poker moment had arrived. Lobke looked at the map and listened to what I had to say. I tried to read him. I looked for a spark in his eye, the registering of a connection to someone who'd pay a fortune for my map. Sure enough, there it was – the spark. I tried to read deeper. I'd finished speaking, but Lobke hadn't stopped looking at the map. One corner of his mouth curled ever-so-slightly upward. The name was in his head. That's when a terrible thought occurred to me. Would I call him on it?

— What terrible thought?

— The thought that the name he'd registered was Mad Manny Horstedt.

— God. How could you know that, though? And how would Lobke know of Mad Manny?

— Come on, Saddler. Just because Lobke usually sells shitty Impressionist forgeries doesn't mean he can't make an obvious connection like that. He knows everyone on the dark side of the business. He'd probably thought of it before he'd even seen the map – he'd thought, "Map – Manny." Just as I'd done. So now I had to find out. If I sold Lobke the map and he went to Manny . . .

— I get you. Ill will all around. And one extra middleman.

— I felt trapped. If I gave him Manny's name – well, that wouldn't do. If I let it ride and dealt with Lobke and the map ended up with Manny anyway, I'd have lost.

— Not necessarily. Wouldn't it depend on the price? Lobke probably drives a harder bargain. No offence.

— I know, but I was having to think on my feet. So I came right out and said, "You've thought of a name, haven't you, Mr Lobke?" He said, "Oh, yeah." I went right ahead and told him that for my own reasons I needed to rule out a few people. Naturally, he was several steps ahead of me. "The people you've shown it to," he said. I guess I'd given him the impression that I'd trotted the map all over Europe. Not a good move. "Only one person I need to rule out," I said.

— Why would he care? You'd either deal with him or not.

— Well, at this stage I think Lobke thought I was a more experienced crook than I am, that I fenced things routinely. So what did I do? I told him this was my first time.

— God, you're hopeless. What were you *thinking*?

— I don't know. I just blurted out, "This is a one-off. It's an insanely valuable piece. I need to rule out one name." He put the map down and nodded at me with pity, with a little *disgust*. But he said, "Have it your way. I have *three* names in my head." Now I'm thinking, How desperate is this guy? How are his finances? Does he want to trade up, villa-wise? Can he afford his *manservant*? Is he in trouble with the law? Will he tell me the truth?

— Of course he wouldn't. Jesus.

— He said, "We'll do this step by step." I told him to go on. "All on the Continent," he said. Did that rule out a Swedish tax exile?

— Did that rule out the cardinal?

— Lobke wouldn't go to the *Vatican*, for Christ's sake. Please. Only I'm that stupid.

— All right.

— I told him I needed a little more. Nationality? Lobke thought about whether he should reply, then he said, "The Latin countries." Right there I made a snap decision and I said – these were my exact words – "Name your price."

— Butch, Hart, butch.

— Lobke decided to tell me another story, but I could see he was thinking hard – it was another poker moment. You may have noticed that I am the *worst* negotiator. I reckoned I ought to be paid a premium just for my nerve, my eye, my desperate act.

Where would the professional fence be without his reckless thief? I looked for pertinent allegory in the story Lobke chose to tell. This one was about another society lady. She had systematically stolen art from her husband, to whom she had been married for a quarter of a century. She used her husband's money to pay forgers to copy his art, she stole the originals, she hung the fakes on the walls, she sold the originals for a fortune, over a period of many years. Then she divorced the oblivious husband, and made a great show of letting him keep his paintings, almost all of which by then were fakes. "That," Lobke said, "was my comeback."

— I see no allegory.

— None, unless he was simply saying, "I've done shady deals that would make your head swim, so let's not waste time." Then he named his price.

— . . . ?

— Saddler, he said it with a sigh. The sigh that says, "I wish I could do more." The sigh that says, "This goes against my better judgement." All of that nonsense. What was I going to do?

— You haven't told me—

— Five hundred and fifty-thousand pounds.

— We're rich! You cooly said yes, and we're rich! That's why your hands are trembling. That's why your whole *body* is shaking. It's a triumph. You're a genius. I want to hug you. You won the game. It's over.

— Not . . . quite.

— Oh, no.

— I gave out my own sigh. It said, "I'm so disappointed."

— Hart, really, frankly, fuck you.

— I had no choice.

— But you'd *done* it. You were safe for years. The drama was over. *Please* tell me you didn't turn him down.

— I wasn't going to allow his take-it-or-leave-it attitude. That's never how it's done. You have to be as strong, at least, as the other guy. I told him he had to rethink his offer. I said I would consult the other interested parties and be back to him by Friday afternoon.

— That's *tomorrow,* Hart.

— Is it?

— Oh, aren't we insouciant, all of a sudden. You're a fool. You just got offered, what, ten years' pay even if all went well? You just blew my *swimming pool*?

— I thought you said there was nothing wrong with your swimming pool.

— You'd better have a very good reason for having turned down your crook.

— I'll tell you exactly: what he's offering is not enough. Our map is worth more; if he has half a million or more in hand, he has twice that in a few days; unless I'm going to continue in a life of crime, this is my one shot and I'm not going to short-change myself; I'm going to wait to hear from Manny and the Church experts; I won't be pushed around by an experienced fence like So-So Lobke, who'd be laughing behind my back if I accepted. Now, may I continue? There are a couple of things I still need to tell you.

— Ach. Go ahead. You *arsehole*.

— I thanked Lobke for breakfast and for his offer. I complimented him on his expertise, for having recognised at least *part* of the map's value, and so very quickly. I said I would think about accepting a much higher offer, and I urged him to think about making one. I said I had imminent meetings with my other interested parties, and that we ought to speak again in a few days.

— Did he tell you to fuck off?

— No. He's a civilised crook. He gave me a superior look, implying my inexperience, and agreed to "have a little think" while I continued on my "mission". He said that he'd be interested in a truthful version of my other interested parties' version of the map's value. He also said, "I'm in the enviable position of not really giving a damn." I thought that was all fair enough, and I left on friendly terms. "No matter what happens," he said, "I'd love you to visit me in France."

— Still hitting on you.

— If you say so. Everyone's gay these days.

— Why didn't you ring me straightaway? Do you know how frantic I've been?

— I wanted to. I had to collect my thoughts. I had to walk a long way to find a taxi. I was going to see Sophie.

— Silly man.

— I didn't turn on my phone until I'd been driven back into central London. Didn't want to speak to Mary. I had a couple of hours, so I thought I might drop by Rory's shop, make an appearance. See how the Stenniman show was getting on. When I turned on the phone, it rang in my hand.

— Mary?

— Andreas. Lots of background noise. It was deep into lunchtime in Munich. He was roaring and laughing into the phone, shouting, "*Hen*ry Hart! *Hen*ry Hart! Can that really be you? You old *shit*, man." He was schoolboy-singing, "Andreas has *some*thing to *tell* you, Andreas has *some*thing to *tell* you." I was paying the driver at the time. I was so distracted by Andreas' call that I almost let the taxi drive away with my briefcase and map still in the back of the cab. Had to pound on the door. I went into a sidestreet so I could hear what Andreas was saying. He was obviously dining in his own whisky bar, with plenty of friends. "Can you hear me, Henry Hart? Can you hear the cele*bra*tions?" I told him I could hear the celebrations, but that if he wanted to talk to me he had to go somewhere quiet. "I'm locking myself in the *toi*let, I'm locking myself in the *toi*let!" I had a terrible feeling I knew what he was going to say.

— I have that feeling now. The Hawaii?

— Good for *you*, Saddler. Good for *you*. "Andreas has sold the Hawaii. Andreas has sold the Ha*wa*ii."

— Bastard.

— That's what I said. I'm not so sure I ever liked Andreas. He knew perfectly well he was talking about the map that had *broken* me. The Hawaii was the turning point. And now, to gloat this way? "Andreas has sold the Ha*waii*." It's no excuse that he was drinking and celebrating with his friends. He was being cruel. I told him to quieten down and give me facts. "Oh, mister *business*man," he said. I'll just give you the upshot, Saddler, and you can take it as read that he was singing and taunting his way through this.

— OK.

— Andreas was obsessed by that Hawaii, more than I'd ever been. I'd had to write it off. I knew damned well it was a copy. The Jap's people had made sure I knew that. But Andreas, who'd bought out my share for three grand – at that time I thought it a lifesaving sum – couldn't let go. He hadn't hung it on the wall as a dartboard. Not at all. He'd tried to beat the Japs at their own research. He *willed* the map to be valuable. After a couple of years he found what he needed. The map was a copy, all right, but it was doctored. It had been used to eliminate a whole island. You'd have to know more about Hawaii than I even *want* to know, but when Andreas noticed there was an island missing, he had an anomaly, a bit of history. He found out who made it, and why. You're probably asking yourself, who would delete an island?

— Yes.

— The story Andreas tells makes sense. You delete an island from a map, and ships run aground. You are some sort of pirate, in other words.

— This makes it valuable?

— Of course. A curiosity. We'd paid a fortune for a very early explorer's map of Hawaii. It proved to be one of many late copies. The map, had it been real, would have been very valuable. When it turned out to be a copy, it was far less so. When it proved to be a copy with history behind it, it was valuable all over again. Now

Andreas had a unique, very old map of Hawaii with a *story* behind it.

— I don't want to be crude, but . . .

— One hundred and thirty thousand pounds.

— He broke roughly even.

— Well, there's breaking even and there's breaking even. He's had what amounts to an unexpected windfall. He's rich again.

— It's not *that* much.

— Enough to get him back in the business, Saddler. And enough to rub my face in it.

— You can't think that way. You did the right thing at the time.

— Pah. What if *I'd* taken the time to notice that there was a whole *island* missing? And why didn't the Japs notice? Or maybe they did, and weren't inclined to tell us. They just didn't want the map. They're hard to read, the Japanese. But how could *I* not have noticed?

— I repeat, you can't think that way. And Andreas did steer you in his friend the cardinal's direction.

— Can't you let me be disappointed? Regretful?

— Sure. Is that the reason you're all a-flutter?

— If only.

— What, then?

— Whew. I'll try to compose myself. I dropped in at Rory's. He wasn't there. I spoke to some colleagues – they're all very suspicious of me. I think they look down on maps. Of all the stuff Stenniman was going to sell, the maps were going to be the bargain basement.

— If only they knew.

— I got out of there, on the double. I decided to buy Sophie a present.

— I thought you didn't give her things.

— This was a first, yes. I was going to walk a good hour to her flat, and buy her something on the way. I was going to pretend I was celebrating something with her. She knew I had something big in the works, though of course I never told her what it was. I wanted to reassure her that the Porter business wasn't on my mind, that I was still committed to our . . . non-commitment.

— Clever.

— I bought Sophie a pin. You know French girls. They wear scarves, jackets. I bought her a subtle gold number that's probably not really from Peru. I justified the cost on the grounds that it was less than ten days' worth of Porter's Sophie extortion, which I had just refused to pay. I charged it to my secret card that Mary doesn't know exists.

— Didn't you think this gesture might make Sophie think you were interested in more than what you've called "exercise"?

— Come on. I was grateful to her. Girls like presents. I wanted her to be happy. I wouldn't say it was a "gesture". It was an offering. I wanted to see her smile, have a good afternoon, return to the trenches. I thought, in fact, that I might use the offering of the pin as a way to say thank you and goodbye. Remember, I was on a high. I'd had an offer on the map, even though I'd temporarily turned it down. I was feeling in control. I was a successful art thief on his way to meet his mistress in the middle of the afternoon. This was a step up from what had gone before. And I was furious with Andreas. This was a form of revenge, getting my mistress a gold pin.

— One way of looking at it.

— I arrived at the steps down to Sophie's flat at exactly half past three. She opened the door before I could knock. For once she didn't leap into my arms. I asked her what was the matter. She said it was nothing, a small problem at work. She said she sometimes felt "used". I wondered, but didn't ask, if this meant she felt used by *me*. I hardly thought so. I said I'd brought her something that might make her feel better. I gave her the pin. We sat on the bed while she opened the box. She really did seem delighted. She hugged me and kissed me, like a girlfriend. She . . . When . . .

— Hart? Are you all right? Hang on. Here. Just . . . What is it?

— Let's . . . move these to the corner. Let's go over there. Come on.

— Jesus. We're fine here. It's fine. No one's looking. Do you want a glass of water? Just take a breath, for God's sake.

— . . . When . . . I'd given her the pin, and she started to kiss me, and she said she didn't want to talk anymore, she wanted to make love. I thought, you know, what a great girl. What a distraction she'd been. I . . . I liked her a lot. We were undressing each other. Then she said, "Let me close the curtains." And I said, "Let me." And then I thought to myself that the curtains had never been open before, not that I really remembered. I'd already stood up. I went around the bed, naked, over to the one window. Doing that, I had a little twinge, recalling looking out of the window at Annette. I reached up to feel for the cord, and I looked outside . . . Aw, Saddler . . .

— Take a breath.

— It was *Mary*. Face pressed between the bars. Staring right at me, a foot away . . .

— . . .

— She . . .

— Just hold on, calm down. Take a minute. I'll get us a drink.

— . . .

— Thanks, Saddler. While you were at the bar I went to splash my face. I'm better. I'm OK.

— No, you're not. Can you tell me what happened, then?

— Sure. Sure. Whew. You know, I just . . . Here's what I saw. Mary's face, inches away. I could tell she'd been there for some time. Probably she'd followed me, or *obviously* she'd followed me – how else . . .? Just as I'd suspected all along, her and Porter ganging up on me. So she'd been at the bottom of the stairs, looking into the room, since I got there. She'd seen everything – greeting, gift of pin, kissing, undressing . . . Whew.

— Come on, Hart. What did you *do*?

— Oh, I don't know, silent scream? Feeling of falling through hole in ground? Own life and faces of daughters flashing before eyes? All in the instant it took Mary to turn and clatter up the stairs.

— You ran after her?

— Of course not. I wasn't dressed, for one thing. And for another, there was Sophie to deal with. I turned round, probably clawing fingernails down my own cheeks, and she was calmly arranging herself on the bed and reaching out for me.

— You didn't.

— For once, you're right. I was all flight instinct, and was already pulling on my clothes as I shouted at her that my *wife* had been looking in through the window. Now, you'd think that would get her attention, that she'd flip and start jumping about the room in horror. But she didn't. What did she do? She accused me of imagining things. She said, "I know you feel guilty, but honestly . . ." I was breathing hard, tripping over my trousers, hopping on one foot. I might have fallen down, I don't know.

— Panic.

— Goddamned right, panic. But what was I going to do? You don't rehearse this scene. Mary would be long gone. I wasn't going to try her phone, was I. Was I supposed to go home, talk it out? All I could do was get dressed, tell Sophie I wasn't imagining things, apologise to her, tell her I'd ring her when it was all sorted out, pathetically thank her for being such a good girlfriend, grab my coat and bolt.

— Where to?

— Good question. It was lonely, out there in the street. It was, what, four o'clock in the afternoon? It was too cold to simply find a spot to sit while I thought out my options – not that I had many. I reckoned I only had one chance here, what with my being so completely in the wrong.

— What was that?

— I had to find out that Mary was having an affair. To cancel out my own.

— I'm amazed that you were so clinical.

— I'm foreshortening. Obviously throwing myself under a bus came first. And plenty of other things, all to be ruled out, in a few minutes' time, before settling on the idea that if, in the next hour or so, I could *prove* that Mary was having an affair too, that all would be well.

— . . . ?

— Don't look at me that way. I'd had my suspicions. There are often hours at a time when Mary's not with the girls. I thought, you know, she could be having a long-term *proper* extramarital affair, she could be in *love* with someone, unlike me with my accidental, hour-at-the-gym, meaningless, loveless, sporadic, wholly non-spiritual liaison with Sophie. I thought she was having an affair with Porter.

— Mary had seen you give Sophie a gift.

— Thanks, Saddler. Yes, she had. A *parting* gift, is what I would explain, from my knees.

— Did you get that chance?

— No. I did not. I went to a fucking pub – you know, just to make sure I ticked the box next to every cliché available to me, so that I could mutter to myself with the other wretches. I reckoned if I found a quiet corner where I could be warm and have a drink, I could speak aloud to myself, give me some auto-advice, prepare my line of defence. The moment I got into that position, I started to focus. And what did I focus on? Have a guess.

— . . . Porter.

— Exactly. Porter's revenge for my having refused to pay the Sophie part of his extortion. It was a power play.

— Did it help you, with Mary, to focus on Porter?

— Not in the slightest. But, man of action that I have become, the thought of – I don't know – *murdering* Porter was a way of distancing myself from the crisis on the home front. How, where and when would I murder Porter? After killing him, and only after killing him, I could rationally explain to Mary that even if she hadn't cancelled out the whole thing by having an affair of her own – which I would never believe – my behaviour fell squarely in the acceptable range of normal husbands' ways of coping with the Existential Mystery.

— Then everything would be fine.

— Right.

— You're crazy.

— Well, what would *you* do?

— Funny, Hart. That's the first time you've asked me any version of that question. I mean, for my real opinion.

— Feel free to reply. But I don't know if I like your tone. Be gentle with me. Try to imagine every little thing you've done that you might regret. Add them up over ten, twenty years. Faux pas, betrayals, lies, taking advantage, cheating in any way, having sex with your *godson*. And say, for the moment, that they aren't cancelled out by acts of charity, well-meant honesty or the purely loving gesture. And those little things – it's a long list, for most people – all fall down. You're busted for everything you've ever done wrong. This is what has just happened to me.

— Ah, forgive me, but that's precisely *it*. "What has just happened to me". In what sense has it "happened" to you? Sorry, I just have to say this now. I've listened to you for all this time and your slant on things seems to be that events occur and you react to them given what you think are limited options. You are the most *selfish* person I know. Poor Mary catches you with another woman, and your almost immediate reaction is to say – and I assume you're only saying this – "I'll murder Porter." This happened, what, a few hours ago? Where's Mary? I'm not asking where she is physically – no doubt she's en route with the children to her mother's, who knows, you aren't telling me – I'm asking where Mary is in your *emotions*. You've said, "You know how I adore Mary." Well, really? Next you'll say, "But she wasn't supposed to find out." A betrayal like yours is an act of violent hatred, whether it's found out or not.

— If you're going to go all tree-falling-in-the-woods on me, I—

— Be quiet. Be *quiet*. You don't have a lot of ammunition left. I'm sick of hearing you defend yourself. You started off this latest phase by talking about our "pact", whatever it can possibly mean to either of us now. Is this how you live up to it? You're the one who married. You're the one who started a family. You're the one who got wrapped up in Annette. You're the one who stole the map. You're the one who started an affair with a much younger French girl. You're the one who got caught. You're the one who boasts that you'll hold your head high on the way to the cells, who says that "people" will say, "He's *done* it." You've *done* it, all right. Jesus.

— . . .

— Stop. This . . . this *philosophy* you think you live by. What is it? It was supposed to be freedom, and you've ended up lashing out at fat cats and behaving like a cornered animal. I mean, either you let go, or you don't. Do you want to be an outlaw? I've said I'll help you. I *want* to help you. Stick to what you believe, go ahead. I *agree* with you. But don't tell me things have gone wrong when you're exposed. You're doing what you think is right. The consequences, therefore, are acceptable to you. Where's Mary?

— I assume she's at home. She's not . . . answering.

— And your plans for the evening?

— Going home is out of the question.

— Are you asking if you can stay with me?

— Wouldn't want to put you *out*, Saddler. But if I could just have the one night, I think I have a plan.

— I can't wait to hear it.

— According to my plan, I am at this moment having a nervous breakdown. For all we know this is true. I have come to you in distress. I need until tomorrow afternoon, after my meetings with the experts and my meeting with Manny and my phone call to Lobke.

— You're still thinking about *that*?

— It would explain everything. I make my loot, tell Mary all, explain the stress of the outlaw's life, beg her forgiveness.

— That's what you want?

— Simple, no? I'll have had an adventure; I'll rid myself of debt, my family will be safe; Mary will *look up* to me for having taken such a gamble; I'll be back in the business. I might even do the whole thing again, don't you see?

— And my role in this is to confirm that you've had a nervous breakdown?

— That, and to make a couple of hundred thousand or more. There's that to think about.

— Oh, believe me, I do.

— And there's one *tiny* bit of information you don't yet have.

— Which is?

— On my way here I heard from old Cambon. I'd kept the phone on just in case, you know, Mary . . . Cambon's so *good* about checking in. That's what we want in our detectives.

— What did he want?

— Cambon would like to have a word with me.

— So? You were talking to him.

— He wants to see me in person, in St-Vuis. This is for my benefit, he says. Doesn't want to raise any dust. So I was thinking . . . You know, after tomorrow, when we know more about the map. We might, you and I . . .

— Go to my place in France?

— That's right. It all fits. I've had my nervous breakdown. I throw myself on the mercy of my old friend Saddler. I leave the country to reassemble myself. I am ashamed, deeply troubled. I don't want anyone to know where I am. If Mary speaks to you, you tell her this story. You say there are reasons why she mustn't tell *anyone* where I am. You eventually admit that I've been hospitalised on the Continent, but you won't say where. Do you still have a car in this country?

— Yes.

— Will you do me yet another favour and stash the Pilgrim Map at your flat after I show it around tomorrow?

— Sure.

— I was thinking, then, a late ferry for France tomorrow night?

*The following day, en route from London to France, by car*

— Isn't this *fun*, Saddler?

— You tell me.

— I've taken the battery out of my phone. We're headed towards the open sea. No one knows where we are. Glorious.

— Do you have your passport?

— Of course I do, *Mother*. I thought I might need it at any moment to prove my identity to the shysters we've been dealing with.

— And?

— Well. My news is a bit all over the place. I can't guarantee you a conclusion just yet. And I'm on very little sleep. Are we headed for Dover?

— Yes.

— Jolly *good*. You have to admit, Saddler, that we're on an adventure. You don't get *this* every day.

— I can't deny that.

— Will we make our ferry?

— With a minute to spare, at least.

— Now, first things first. Tell me the truth. Have you spoken to Mary?

— I haven't. Have you?

— No. Even if she were at home, and answering the phone, which I doubt, it wouldn't fit with our plan if I were to speak to her. Remember, I've had a nervous breakdown. A nervous breakdown that *preceded* her finding me in flagrante. What she saw through those bars and that window was a husband already consumed by stress. It will all make sense. Where will we stay tonight?

— If you get some sleep, you can help me drive. We'll go all the way.

— I love your attitude, Saddler.

— . . .

— Now, don't fume. I know you're enjoying this. We ought to have done it years ago. Let's take a look at our assets. How much cash have you got?

— I have more than three hundred euros in cash.

— With my tenner added on top, we're in business for at least three or four days. Is the ferry paid for?

— Yes.

— That would mean you have credit.

— Some.

— Excellent, Saddler. I'll reimburse you in spades, promise.

— Good.

— Now. I have not been an idle boy today. My first appointment was with the cardinal's experts. You'd think they would have wanted to take the map away, get the electron microscopes, scour secret libraries, meet at a lab of some sort in – I don't know, Bletchley Park? But no. They wanted an hour. And they wanted to be alone with the map. I don't even know how many of them there were. I showed up at the address, a mews house not a million miles from Connaught Square. Who was there to greet me?

— Father Anthony.

— Correct. Only he wasn't wearing his habit.

— Hart . . .

— OK. He wasn't wearing his *fulmination*. I don't know what it's called.

— Dog collar.

— That's what he wasn't wearing. He was all business. The very first thing he said to me was, "Hello, Mr Hart." Meaning that they'd checked up on me and they knew I'd lied about my name.

— Bad?

— Good. Cloak and dagger. Confirmed their shady motives and their interest in the map. So it was as simple as this: I handed over the map to Father Anthony, who asked me to wait in the vestibule. I sat on a little chair. I wasn't even offered tea. It was like waiting outside a doctor's office. An hour later Father Anthony came back with the map. I took a *good* look at it, to make sure they hadn't switched it on me. Father Anthony said that he would be in touch. I said that might be difficult – thinking ahead, Saddler, thinking ahead. I said I would contact him by telephone in a week, back in Rome. This was fine with Father Anthony. I asked him if he could tell me anything right away, because of the other interested parties. He did that conspiratorial, gay thing with his mouth – sorry – and looked over his shoulder to make sure no one could overhear, and he said, "*Very* positive, I'm certain of it."

— Hurrah.

— Next stop, Mad Manny. I had plenty of time to get there on foot. I knew I had to knock on his door *precisely* at noon so as not to disturb his routine. That's how considerate I am. Same as the previous time, the weather turned as I approached his house. I was walking down the Gloucester Road, in fine cold sunshine, and when I took a right into St Alban's Grove it began, I swear, to rain – no, *sleet*. Mrs Horstedt – that would be the rather gorgeous old Martha – answered the door before I'd fully withdrawn my fist from knocking just the once. As before, she escorted me through Manny's submarine door to the gloomy library and left me alone with her husband. I mentioned that it was sleeting outside, and Manny looked at me as if I'd said the city had been destroyed by a nuclear attack. Perhaps I'd triggered a memory of Sweden? I placed the map on his desk and he soon calmed down. On my way over there I'd decided to tell him, right off, about the Vatican. I wasn't going to mention So-So Lobke, but I thought that telling him about the cardinal might help our cause.

— You weren't afraid this would make him angry? Sounds a jittery sort.

— There was that risk. I went for it anyway. I said, "I've come, just now, from a group of Vatican experts who are very interested in my map." Manny didn't bat an eye. He simply nodded, looking down at the map on his desk, as if he'd known this information already.

— You're just going to string me along, aren't you. You enjoy teasing me.

— I want you to *experience* our crime.

— Fine. I've had the sleet, I've had the gloom. Does he want the map?

— You know, Saddler, if I wanted to I could try to relate, word for word, what Manny said to me during the next hour. I will spare you that, because you seem to be so impatient. Manny's a bit of a mumbler. He didn't go back through the list of his lifetime's acquisitions again, thank God, but he began to mutter about metal engraving, the difficulty of dating silver, the lack of precedents for such an object as mine. He quite obviously has a photographic memory, because he started to list features of my map that I'd have to go back with the magnifying glass and search for myself. He'd snapped the thing with his weird brain. He'd obviously been thinking about little else. So he went on, in his Swedish accent, *mut*ter *mut*ter *mut*ter.

— Did he *mut*ter a *fuck*ing *off*er?

— In fact . . .

— Well?

— In fact, he *mut*tered a *fuck*ing *off*er – of *se*ven *hun*dred *thous*and *pounds*.

— Ah! We're rich again! So you leaped to your feet, shook the old man's hand, danced about the room, toasted him with berry wine, kissed old Martha, gave him your bank details, left them with the map as a show of good faith?

— Er . . . no.

— I'll say it again. You are *so* impossible.

— Maybe. What's the weather going to be like in France?

— Clear blue and warmer than this shit.

— I was thinking about the first time we were in France together. I remember coming up out of the Gare du Nord and having to run to keep up with you. It was as if you'd lived there before, you knew it all so well.

— I'd done a lot of reading. Why are you changing the subject?

— There's something I've always wanted to ask you. You probably don't even remember this, the way I do.

— Try me.

— This wasn't so long after the events at Nathan's funeral and the days I spent with your family. So the pact was fully in force. And I suppose, from your parents' point of view – not Lily's obviously, I'd been sleeping with her – you were off on a quick summer break with your . . . boyfriend. Is that what they thought?

— Yes, it is.

— OK, fine. That first day was *wild*. I don't think I've ever walked so far in my life. You were very much the tour guide, and the guide to the nightlife. I thought you *knew* all of those people we fell in with. In a café I'd go to the loo and come back to find you surrounded by beautiful older boys and girls – that's to say, in their early twenties. You did say to me, "Small world," and I honestly assumed these people were at least acquaintances.

— I was outgoing in those days.

— What a *swirl* it became. I'd never had so much fun. One minute we're eating oysters on someone's terrace in Les Halles, the next we're looking at African art in someone's gallery, suddenly it's dark and everyone's watching a show – what beautiful women those men made. Dancing, champagne. And I thought, "This is Saddler's world?" I also thought, "Who's paying for all this?" I assumed it was the Norwegian man, who was older. And the girls! I know they probably thought I was a child, but they were – mmm, they were . . . I remember every one of them – their teeth, their hair, their slender arms. It *hurts*, to remember them. And one of them, a French girl who seemed so mature but in retrospect must have been twenty-two years old, who gave me her hat? It was a straw hat, maybe a girl's version of a Panama. It didn't really fit me, so I wore it at an angle. I thought, "This girl loves me." So I danced and laughed with her. Do you remember any of this?

— Not from that point of view.

— I was wearing her hat and dancing with her – and dancing with a few half-naked black men, as I recall. Legitimately drunk on life. I waved the hat in the air. I have no idea what part of town we were in by that time. Some sort of fashion show burst on to the stage. Crazy lights and explosions. When the sparklers were extinguished, and it was time to move on, I couldn't find the girl who'd given me her hat. Everyone rushed into the streets. You and I were together, I still had the hat, but there was no girl. People vanished into the night. You and I walked. You do remember this part, don't you?

— Yes.

— We got to the river. I was so excited, but also disappointed that the girl had got away. I didn't even know her name. I complained about this to you, and you . . . you put your arm around my shoulder. You didn't say anything, but I supposed you were consoling me, you were giving me a squeeze to say, "There'll be other girls." So with a great sigh I stopped, in the middle of the bridge, and looked out at what was very soon going to be a sunrise. You stopped with me. That's when you reached over and took the girl's hat off my head, you looked at it, then you flipped it into the air so that it twirled down, down into the Seine. You *do* remember that?

— Yes, I do.

— And therefore you would remember kissing me.

— Yes. I remember that we kissed each other.

— Except that it wasn't really a *kiss.*

— No? More of a . . . a meeting of the lips?

— That's more like it. Not very romantic.

— Oh, certainly not. Kissing on a bridge over the Seine. It's not as if we *held hands* or anything. Just the kiss.

— Don't be cruel, Saddler. I wasn't myself. I was busy being in love with that French girl, who will live forever in my memory.

— Unlike our kiss.

— I don't mean that. But I remember I asked you about her just then. I thought you knew her.

— I didn't know her.

— I'm saying I *thought* you did. And I guess I wondered why you'd thrown her hat into the river.

— I didn't think it suited you.

— Well, here's something else. We went back to that little hotel. We hadn't even checked in properly that day. Our bags were still downstairs. We woke up the concierge and got our key. We went upstairs and found that there was just the one bed. Now, Saddler, keep in mind – and please, please try to believe me – I still really had no idea about you. Don't roll your eyes. You were my friend. We'd already known each other ten years, and somehing like that was a huge adjustment. I'll admit it was *dawning* on me, slowly, but I was just playing along. It was too foreign. So I'm sorry for what I said. Do you remember what I said?

— Ha. Of course. You looked at that one bed. You dropped your bag on the floor and you said, "Now's your chance, Saddler."

— I was pretending to be grown up. And I'm sorry. Saying that has haunted me ever since.

— It's OK, Hart.

— You weren't—

— You should probably drop this line. It isn't necessarily important.

— I just wanted to clear things up. I do have a way of gnawing on the past. It bothered me.

— Look, you rolled into bed, very courageously, and passed out. That's it. I rolled in right next to you and, eventually, did the same.

— No, you didn't.

— What?

— Saddler, I slept for about two hours, and when I opened my eyes you weren't there. You never slept in that bed.

— Oh.

— I even went down the hall and looked for you in the shower. You weren't there. You'd left.

— That's possible. It was a long time ago.

— Twenty years, yes. But I still remember. I went downstairs to the little dining room. You weren't there, either. So I thought . . . I'll tell you what I thought. I thought you'd gone out to meet the girl. That you had an arrangement with her to spare my feelings. Remember, I thought you knew her. I was sure you'd gone to see her that morning. I was pretty angry. I went back upstairs and got back into bed and waited for you to come back. Which you did, at about ten o'clock in the morning. You thought I was asleep. You pretended you'd been sleeping there next to me.

— Oh, I *deceived* you, did I?

— Well, yes. And I spent all day being furious because I thought you'd been with the girl.

— You cannot *possibly* have thought that.

— For a while I really did. I guess I finally figured out where you'd gone.

— Let's hear it.

— You went off to see the Norwegian guy.

— Well done.

— I knew it. Why didn't you *tell* me? Wouldn't that have been easier?

— Hart, you've got to remember there were a certain number of games being played. I was getting used to what I was suddenly allowed to do. I didn't want you to know that's what I did.

— Why not?

— Well, first you stay with me and my family, then you go off to Paris with me, dance the night away in a gay club –

— I didn't.

— – kiss me on a bridge, say "Now's your chance," hop into our bed . . . And then you go to sleep. So I went out to see my new friend, out of revenge. I didn't want you to know because I thought maybe I was *cheating* on you. All right? Can we stop talking about this? You're avoiding something, Lobke-wise. I can tell.

— I'm too tired for this. I'll tell you on the ferry.

— You'll tell me now.

— Oh, look, they're already letting the cars on board. You *are* an expert getaway driver.

— Tell me.

— In the morning. In France. When we're safe. I'm so tired. Take me to bed, Saddler.

— . . .

— Where are we?

— According to the milometer, Hart, we're three hundred and sixteen miles into our journey, plus the ferry crossing. You slept like a dead man and hardly woke up when I helped you back down to the car. It is four o'clock in the morning. We are travelling at nearly eighty miles an hour. Feeling all right? I'll get us a coffee. Perhaps you'd like to drive? I've reached my limit. I'd like to curl up in the back.

— . . .

— Saddler? You're home now.

— Good work. What time is it?

— Just past eight in the morning. I took an accidental detour off the *autoroute*. Goodness me, look at this. It's even more grand than I remembered.

— Oh, stop it. Let's get you a jumper and have a look around.

— You leave the place unlocked?

— Someone comes round to lock up at night. That sound you hear is a cement mixer. My crack *équipe* must be on site. They have the run of the house. Here, take this jacket. Let's see what the boys are up to. This way. You remember, don't you?

— I know the way to the stables.

— Of course you do. Oh, look, it's Alban. Come here, Alban. Look how you've grown. No, Alban won't come. He's the *worst* kind of kitten.

— There are male kittens?

— You're going to learn a lot, out here in the countryside. There are my boys. I'm calling that a patio. Shall we say good morning?

— You go ahead. I'm supposed to be in hiding. I'll find my way back to the kitchen. There might be tea.

— . . .

— The boys have pronounced themselves satisfied with their work. Did you find milk? Come through, we need a fire. If you want a rest, feel free. I'm putting you in the Blue Room. I can dash out for supplies. My clothes will fit you. Sit. You have to give me a little more information, Hart, if we're going to plan ahead. And by the way, do you mind if I call you Henry? The surnames are getting a little forced now that we're living together.

— What do I call you?

— You can be very formal and call me Darius. Now then. About So-So Lobke.'

— You won't even let a chap settle in? And, if you'll remember, our discussions have always been washed down with a little something.

— I'll allow us a glass of red, on account of the chill, and you will *tell* me.

— Thanks, *Darius*. You pour, I'll talk. I love this room, by the way. It must be a hell of a feeling to be able to exercise one's own taste. I have never, in my life, lived in a room made to my own liking. Not ever. It's a pitiful way to live. Right here, I wouldn't change a thing. I can put my feet up?

— That's what they're for.

— I suppose, when you're alone, you can sit here and read a book? Heaven. At my house, if I want to read a book, I have to lock myself in the downstairs loo. Oh, thank you. Yes, that's good. And a real fire. This is overwhelming luxury. You'll have to take me on a tour. I don't see that you have too much more work to do. But what a shame to sell.

— I have a banker you could talk to about what a shame that would be. And the work is endless. I'll stop when the plumbing stops complaining. My plumber's mother died. Patrice's in a foul depression. If he shows up he only makes things worse, then he bursts into tears. If I sacked him he'd kill himself. So here we are.

— Yes. Here we are. And I've had some time to think, driving you all the way down to your lovely home. I've had a chance to prioritise. Here's how I see things. As you say, "Here we are." And in some ways, here is where it all started. A year and a bit ago. When I—

— Yes, yes . . .

— No, it's something else. I said I was, in a way, *primed* by what I saw out in your broken-down stables, but it was more than that.

— What could possibly have been more than that?

— An earthquake.

— Yes, Henry?

— Not *your* earthquake. An earthquake in Turkey. It happened a couple of months before my visit. My brother –

— I've been meaning to ask about Colin. What a beautiful man.

— – casually asked me if I'd like to hop on a plane and help some freezing, starving Turks on some collapsed slope of rubble.

Well, who wouldn't? And why do you call him a "beautiful man"? I can't recall your ever having met him.

— Oh, but I did. Whether you like it or not, your brother Colin is a magnet. He is, vicariously, a winner of the Nobel Peace Prize. I love what he does with his thinning hair. I met him at a dinner party. He had to leave before the main course. Something to do with Eritrea, I think.

— Thanks, that's the man. I'd been to Turkey before. It's a matter of getting on the old transport and finding yourself in Izmir. Squid, that sort of thing. Except this time I was with *Colin,* and we landed in the middle of nowhere, and the next thing you know I'm on a helicopter being taught how to say, "You're going to be just fine," in Turkish. Already I was being treated like a child. Colin was trying to make a man of me, I suppose. "You'll need a coat, here you go." And Colin rushing about, already with a coat on, and I realise we've landed, we're there. We're where the suffering people are. Well, *fuck*. This is awfully good. I'm going to need a nap in a moment.

— Here.

— Thanks. And I thought I wouldn't get swept up in the thing. You know, Colin's world. Masochist. Flies in to an act of God just so he can be more attractive to women. That is the only possible explanation. I mean, he was his doctor father's doctor son. Some god-like no doubt former IDF helicopter pilot *flings* you into a landing on the mountainside. What do you do to impress? Our father sat on his arse for thirty-five years listening to people who'd finally admitted they had a sneeze. And his son was setting bones as soon as the people were dragged out from under the concrete. Or staring into a camera to tell the world that it actually was rather hellish where he happened to be, holding a token baby in his arms for effect.

— And so you fled.

— The hell I fled. I was right on Colin's heels. You're going to say I was a coward. The *hell* I was. I won't bore you, here in your chateau, but I was plopped down in a place – I mean, Turks don't deserve this bullshit. What was my job? Did I do my job? It was all very quiet. I spent most of my time erecting tents. My brother was doing things with people's chests. If you aren't killed in an earthquake, I don't care how Turkish you are, your chest is going to be a problem. So Colin rushes about being a hero while I try to pound stakes into little metal rings to make the tents go up. Did I mention the blankets? Go to the truck, fetch the blankets, go to the truck, fetch the blankets. Did *I* win a Nobel prize? No, I did not. And I found that I was repelled. I insist I'm not a coward, but I just didn't *like* to see people suffering, the way I suspect my brother does. We'll just have to leave it to people like Colin to set the bones. Well and good that people like Colin are around. We can't all be like him. So I made my excuses, over in poor Turkey, and then I came down here to watch you seduce your godson.

— That really bothered you, didn't it?

— Being here now, it's vivid in my mind.

— If you're going to blame all of your troubles on earthquake victims who rattled you, and Sam in the stables—

— There is no blame. There is only action. We must act, right now, on several fronts. Are you ready? Good. The first thing you do is ring Mary. You'll do it from town. Get us some of those phone cards. We won't be ringing anyone from here. You tell Mary I've had my nervous breakdown at last – you saw it coming, I'm in good hands, that sort of thing. You claim still to be in England. Then I ring Lobke. Get an answer. Sell the Pilgrim Map once and for all. I drive down to St-Vuis and see what Cambon wants. We can disregard Porter from now on; he can't reach me. We will *disengage* him. If he bothers Mary, that might be another story. I happen to think he will go away. Are you following all of this?

— I should probably be taking notes. I believe I was in Turkey for a moment there, wasn't I? I think you need a rest, Henry.'

— One thing at a time. I'm very happy to step out for some fresh air. Do you walk or drive, going into town?

— I have a motorcycle.

— Off we go, then. Call Mary when we're there, please. Stop off for a little *sex*, if you must. I'll sit quietly in the local.

— Through here.

— Oh, nice. What do you call this, then?

— I call her Esmeralda. We don't need helmets. Obviously.

— What, is she electric? This is the silliest motorcycle I've ever seen. Do we have to pedal?

— Tight behind me now, don't be embarrassed.

— . . .

— You reached my darling wife, I take it?

— She was at home.

— Please tell me I was hallucinating at Sophie's place.

— Unfortunately, no, you weren't. That really was Mary. She sounded as if she'd pulled herself together, though. Your daughters were there. They say, "Hi, Daddy."

— Oh, stop.

— I did what you asked me to do. I told her you'd come straight to me – she knew we'd been seeing more of each other. That you'd come to stay at my flat. That you were in a wild state.

— You said that? You said "wild state"?

— I chose those words, yes. Then I was more clinical. I described the emotional breakdown you've been having, for at least a year that I knew of. I said she must surely have noticed, and she said she had. I said I thought it was mainly the pressure of your business, and that you had a big deal in the works. I told her I didn't know who your girlfriend was, but that you'd told me she was an evil temptress who'd taken advantage of your . . .

— Wild state?

— Yes.

— What was her tone? Did she buy this? Was she particularly . . . I don't know, *angry*?

— I know you want me to say she was full of concern for your welfare and your mental health. But, no. Furious is what she is. She didn't even want to know where you are, so I didn't need to lie directly on that score. I think I managed to give her the idea that we were in London. That I was getting you looked after by a doctor friend. That is the kind of thing you wanted, right?

— It's good enough for now. Please talk me through it. We're ticking things off our list. I'm next on the phone, to Lobke, you know. Lovely place, this café, by the way.

— She asked after *me*, actually. She wanted to know how things were going, what with the Sam brouhaha. Her manners are intact, in other words. She did not ask me to elaborate too much after I'd told her about your wild state. She said that she would be grateful if I could keep her posted, but that she would not be expecting to hear from you.

— Well, good, then. This sounds good. Sensible, darling Mary. She's seen the broader picture. Good *girl*. I knew this was going to happen. Christ, she's super.

— She did add that she's divorcing you.

— Oh dear. That's very grown-up of her.

— You have to face this, Henry. She's had enough.

— Pah.

— She has. She only needed an excuse. She's going to start again. What are you going to do?

— I'm going to carry on in my wild state and not believe what you're telling me. Mary will come round. I'll just go and make that call to Lobke, if you don't mind.

— Suit yourself. From what you've said, I doubt he'll be up and about on a Sunday morning.

— . . .

— Did you reach him?

— Hmm?

— Lobke – did you reach him?

— *That's* a rather nice-looking patisserie. I think I might have one, too. Ah, the slender fellow at the bar has caught my eye. Is absolutely everyone gay in your village?

— It has that reputation. And keep your voice down. What about the call?

— Are you and the waiter an item?

— No, and please – ah, *merçi*, Christophe. Here, Henry, eat something for heaven's sake.

— I said before, you know, thank you for not dying. During the Dark Time. I don't know what I'd do without you.

— And I said you're welcome.

— But *how* did you survive? How did you escape?

— Who says I did?

— *What?'*

— Who says I escaped?

— Jesus. You didn't? I mean, you're . . . ?

— No. No, I'm not. Don't worry, I'm OK. It's just that I always found it strange that you never really *asked*, Henry. Inconsiderate. To tell you . . . the truth.

— Well, then, I'm sorry. I'm truly sorry. I can see you're upset.

— I'm not *upset*; I want to know what Lobke said. Jesus, Henry. You're all over the place.

— All right. I'll be as direct as I can be. I've just had an interesting chat with So-So Lobke, with whom it was probably never a good idea to get involved. What does he know about maps, anyway? When I went to see him he hardly looked at the map, and made an enormous offer on the spot. So we shouldn't be surprised that Lobke has changed his tune. He was always intending to strong-arm me, I'm sure of that. He's an angry man with a lot of experience and a *hideous* greed.

— As I recall he offered you more than half a million. To what extent has he changed his mind?

— Not . . . totally. He hasn't slammed the door, if that's what you're asking. But that's not really the news I need to tell you. I'm still trying to figure out what it could mean. Anyway, here goes:

Lobke said, "There's a new issue." I asked him what that would be. In his rambling way – I thought the phone card would run out – he got to the point, after having told me a story about the old days when this sort of thing was more of a gentleman's game, and done ever so transparently. He said, "I got a call from a man named Porter. Ring a bell?"

— Oh, god*damn* it.

— I immediately said that I knew the name but had never met the man. I came right out and said that Porter was some sort of madman who'd been physically and telephonically stalking me, and had nothing to do with the Pilgrim Map.

— Good on you, Henry.

— And then Lobke said, "Your friend Porter knows where the map is from." And I said, "Well, it comes from France, something like eight hundred years ago." And Lobke said, "Porter mentioned an Englishman named Stenniman. Is this someone I should know about, too?"

— You denied you knew him. Please say you denied it.

— Well, I couldn't, could I? Not with Stenniman's whole stash now chez Rory Fine, my employer. I simply said Porter wasn't his real name, I had no idea who he was, and I'd been bothered by him for some time. I said Porter sounded like some sort of stalker, but that I wasn't afraid of him and nor should Lobke be. I said, "I'll bet he spoke in a foreign accent. He's always someone different-sounding." And Lobke said, "Is that so? If that's the case, he does an awfully good well-educated-English accent. I would say that would be almost impossible to fake so well."

— Porter was English-English this time?

— Apparently so. Lobke said they had "an amusing chat". Of course I was dying to know what Porter had chatted so amusingly about, but I had to pretend I didn't care. I just said, "What about my map?" Then Lobke asked me about my bank details. I swear to God. He was twisting me around. First he knows Porter, he's busted me, then he's setting me up for another offer, then and there. Bank details. He's about to offer me nothing, I'm sure of it. Saddler – Darius – am I lost?

— Think so.

— Think so, too. I have to get down to logic. It's Sunday, so I can't very well check in with the cardinal. Lobke's stated his case. Manny's just . . . sitting there. I have to get in touch with Cambon. Oh, to hell with it, I'm turning on my phone. Your boyfriend at the bar won't mind? Christophe? Here, who cares? Battery goes in. Press the button. I promise you, it'll ring in my hand. There it goes. Do you hear that? Do you hear that?

— It'll be Porter.

— Hello? Yes? A message. Of course. He says . . . He's Spanish, now. He says, "How is France? My regards to Mister Darius Saddler. Keep the phone on now, OK, amigo?" Did you get that? Did you hear what he said?

— I heard. So keep the phone on. Maybe you should slow down. You're safe here, with me. You need time to think. Let's buzz back to the house.

— I need to see Cambon. I'll need your car.

— Well, you won't be riding Esmeralda; take you five days. Please sleep first.

— Buzz me home, then.

## France, two days later

Darius Saddler's residence. Henry Hart has returned from his meeting with the French detective, Claude Cambon, in St-Vuis.

— Extraordinary man, Cambon. We met at his house. He's on holiday. I met the wife and daughter. They're all tiny. Cambon's aged in just this short time. You know, that big head of his, he seems to have to hold it up with the palm of one hand. What do you call this lovely plant, here?

— Oleander. It's poisonous.

— And this, here?

— That, Henry, is a dwarf palm. It hasn't long to live.

— It looks like Detective Cambon. He took me round his garden, too. His garden is the size of your unfinished patio. Can you get a lot of money for this place? Tell me the truth.

— When I'm done with the *travaux*, and as I bleed the mortgage, I can sell this place for about two million, all of which by that time will be vapour.

— So your chateau is worth . . . nothing?

— To the penny.

— What about your other houses?

— Free and clear. I could make half a million euros. I was thinking, when this is all over, that you might like to buy one of them. We can walk there from here, while you're telling me about what Cambon had to say.

— Excellent. I'm interested. Oh, look, a little crumbling *bridge*. Let's pause to listen to the purling of the stream.

— The irrigation ditch.

— You're not going to try to kiss me, this time?

— . . .

— I didn't think so. What is this rubble we are looking at, here?

— This, Henry, is my chapel. It is the house of the Lord. If you want to make yourself useful during your stay, you can help me dispose of the stones. It's a ritual I have. I don't walk past here without carrying away a rock or two. A staircase is being made of them. Why did Cambon want to see you again?

— He wanted to see me to *see* me, I think. Or that's what I thought at first. He wanted to stare into my guilty eyes. He wanted to solve his murder case. He was experiencing that awkward position detectives can be caught in, half hoping for another murder to connect the dots. No other murder has come along. At least, not like Annette's. He's had the odd rape, an instantly solved stabbing – oh, and the body of the lesbian's husband turned up. She had nothing to do with that, he'd killed himself way out of town. So Cambon's been a busy little sleuth. But the Annette case was cold, cold, cold, and he wanted another look at me, his only suspect, the English wanker. He took me to lunch – isn't he odd? He took me to a small garden restaurant, the sort of place that's right in the centre of town but you'd have to know about to find. One of the first things he said to me was that he wanted me to stay for a night in the same room in the same hotel where I'd stayed the year before and seen Annette. He said he'd arranged for me to stay there for free. He wanted me to walk where I'd walked, drink where I'd drunk, sleep where I'd slept, and see if I didn't remember something, anything about that night.

— He was fucking with you. He thinks you killed her.

— Yes. Or at least, he *hopes* I killed her, and that I'll suddenly blurt out the truth in a vomitudinous fit of guilt. He's a nervous little guy, Cambon, and I think very clever. We'd just dug into our *carottes rapées* when he suddenly leaned forward and said, "I have only the least bit of information, and so I have to ask, did Annette have a slight limp?" And I immediately replied, "Why, yes, you're right!" I was trying to congratulate him on having triggered my memory, I was flattering him. And it was true. The girl did have a slight limp. I said to him, "Maybe this experiment you're talking about *can* work." I was implying that he was a genius. And then I realised what I'd just admitted. I'd basically confessed that I'd followed Annette.

— Had you? Followed her?

— I'm not sure "followed" is the right word. I walked in the same direction. At some distance. And I wondered why she was limping. That's all, Saddler – *Darius*. Or that's all I told Cambon. I reminded him how hot it was that night, how tired I was, how I'd been drinking too much. And he said, "Well, we've got the limp. Maybe we can get more." I asked him why Annette had been limping. He said she'd injured her foot playing table tennis. By this time I was feeling trapped. I knew he'd go down a line of questioning that would have me following Annette, loitering outside her hotel, spying her coming out to get ice cream, somehow dragging her away towards my hotel, panicking before being able to rape her, strangling her with – who knows, her own shirt? – leaving her in the quad, going back to my room, performing an act of self-love once the sun hit her beautiful naked body.

— That's a long way from noticing that she limped.

— But it's what Cambon must have been thinking. And why wouldn't he? Keep in mind, I *looked* like a child molester at the time. I was hampered by my shitty French. Quick, how do you say "limp" in French?

— Verb, noun or adjective?

— Noun.

— Haven't a clue.

— It's *boîte*. You can imagine the confusion. Did Annette own a nightclub? Was she carrying a box? So I limped onward in my shitty French and got to the point of saying that I had, indeed, walked along well behind Annette and her parents, but not on purpose.

— By this time he's mentally oiling the guillotine.

— No doubt. Except that he had one other shard of information. Something he'd not told me before. Something he'd held in *reserve*, the way cunning detectives do. Of course I was about to throw up my veal at this point, because he was looking at me as if he were about to produce a witness to my crime, or the garrotte with my genetics splashed all over it, and so on. Then he completely changed the subject. He asked me about my family.

— Couldn't you simply have left? Why put yourself through that?

— I wanted to know what he had. I wanted to know how much trouble I might be in. Innocent people are sent down every day. What if he went ahead and tried to pin this on me? And he's got amazing charm, Cambon. When he asked me about my family I sniffed a bit and said that I was in trouble with my wife. I thought, you know, him being a Frenchman, it might chime with his own experience. And that if I showed that I was a proper, grown-up adulterer with marital problems and two small girls, who'd run away to the Continent while things calmed down at home, he might deduce that I in no way fitted the profile of someone who'd attack a child. And if we could just pause here for a second, I can't walk and talk at the same time. How the hell much land do you have?

— Just the five hectares. Right here would be the limit of my property. This is where the tennis court would go, if *someone* would sell his *map*.

— Nice. So Cambon said, "I'll give you my information in a minute. You probably won't mind. But first, may I ask if you know of someone named Porter?"

— Oh, for God's *sake*.

— We can carry on walking now . . . Blimey, is that one of your awful little houses? The one destined to be mine?

— Yes. I thought we'd call it *Coeur de lion*. Heroic, isn't it?

— Seriously, yes, I think it's beautiful. I thought you said it was a ruin.

— The other one is a ruin.

— It's rather glorious, in its tiny, hidden way. How've you done this?

— Seventy thousand quid, give or take. And three and a half years of pleading with and overpaying my labourers. The garden, such as it is, I did myself. What did you *think* I'd been doing? And now will you tell me what Porter had to say this time?

— First of all, I asked Cambon what accent Porter had. Cambon said Porter spoke French well, possibly with a Scandinavian accent, but that he didn't have much to say. Porter gave Cambon his name, said he was *"un ami de Monsieur Henry Hart"*, and that he had a message for the detective. Porter said he knew me well, that he knew I was in France, that he'd been blackmailing me for many months about *l'affaire Annette*, and that I'd been paying up all this time to conceal my involvement.

— When did Cambon get this call?

— The day we came here. Porter knew we ran to France. So now Cambon gets to add to his suspicions the idea that I've been paying blackmail to someone who thinks I killed Annette.

— Porter never said that, did he? He just knew you were there and had . . . embarrassed yourself.

— No, remember, he knew details. I believe more than ever that Mary and her accomplice made them pretty clear to Cambon. And meanwhile, at this strange lunch, Cambon's starting to get a little carried away. Now he was talking about his *own* family, and how he's never been able to "impress" them, how he wants his daughter to think of him as a great detective. His girl knows all about the Annette case – she was the same age. I got the idea that Cambon was disappointed because the Annette case never made big news – too many people dying in the heat wave, the murder just never quite caught on. It's as if he wished Annette *had* been raped, which would have titillated the audience. Then, even if he didn't solve the crime, he would still be on television and his daughter could look up to him. So that's when I interrupted and said, "Perhaps *you* killed Annette, to have a murder to solve." I was being unbelievably clever here, don't you think? "And you tried to pin it on the first vagrant-like masturbator in the vicinity. All to impress your wife and daughter and colleagues." I told Cambon that his admission of wanting fame as a detective was more evidence of his guilt, or at least motive, than anything he had on me.

— You're something, Henry.

— Then I told him to forget about Porter, that Porter was blackmailing me on *two* counts, the other being my sexual affair, that my wife had caught me in the act, and that it was none of his business. I crossed my arms and stared him down. It's so much *work*, being a murder suspect.

— Here, let's go in. I'll play estate agent. This would be sir's kitchen. And through here, sir's *salon*. And further along, the rather splendid room where sir would pull his business back together, after concluding his criminal activities. Upstairs, two beds, two baths and air conditioning throughout – some people don't like that; I insist.

— I love this place. So . . . quiet.

— Here, the original fireplace. It, and its chimney, were what I originally bought. Almost ten years ago, now.

— What would you have done, if your parents hadn't died?

— For money? Very much the same thing, I would have thought. I might have done more, in fact, if I'd had to put my back into it. I probably would have found a friend with money and no drive. We would have come here, or some place like it, and made a life. My career so far is: bought seven properties, sold four. I'm feeling the pressure to work very hard for the next ten years or so, or I'll be sitting right here by the fire with no food to eat and Alban starving to death. There's nothing else I can do. I've been down your way, in St-Vuis, you know. I probably saw some of the same properties you hated so much. They're giving them away. I could turn one around in a year, see some money. The problem is I don't enjoy my job.

— I'm sorry to hear that.

— We can't all be Cambon, you know, swept up in our work, obsessed. What was his new information, the stuff he'd withheld?

— He said he felt stupid and embarrassed for not having found this out immediately after Annette died. He just never asked the right questions. He didn't know, for weeks, that Vincent is not Annette's biological father. He's her stepfather. He married Annette's mother when Annette was just months old, and even some of their relatives didn't know that he wasn't her father.

— I can guess where this leads.

— Yes. Cambon insists that a stepfather is about a trillion times more likely to abuse a stepdaughter than a father is a daughter. That's believable, I'd say, from experience. Now, in order for Vincent to have done the deed, his wife would probably have to know. Their stories were aligned: they came back to the hotel at eleven o'clock, Annette went out for ice cream and never returned. They raised the alarm at about one o'clock in the morning. Cambon finds this a suspiciously late hour. Cambon didn't like the amount of time Vincent had spent looking for his daughter before calling the police. An hour? An hour and a half? He asked himself how long he would search the streets of a foreign town around midnight, looking for his own twelve-year-old daughter, before raising the alarm.

— How long?

— Less than five minutes, he said. So Cambon's got this uncomfortable window – he's got his evil stepfather, he may even have a crazy, complicit wife. Just the fact that Vincent didn't immediately volunteer the information that he wasn't Annette's real father, even given the stressful circumstances, got Cambon excited.

— Let's head back for an aperitif. You look exhausted, Henry.

— Fine. The point is, Cambon now had another suspect, based on nothing more than a gap hour or more, and a non-biological relationship. He had to play this intelligently. He had to assume that Vincent wasn't just going to strangle his stepdaughter out of nowhere. There had to be a history. So Cambon had to talk to the wife. He said he felt terrible doing this, trapping her. I suspect that, on the contrary, he relished the chase. He had to befriend her, show concern, open her up on the pretext of keeping her abreast of his detective progress. He travelled to Paris to meet her, alone. Marie-Laure is her name.

— You've said.

— Naturally, Cambon had to describe this mission as a kind of seduction. He said he had to overcome her Parisian snobbery – and one would think Cambon might be at a disadvantage owing to his small stature. He'd asked Marie-Laure not to tell her husband about their meeting. He said he had questions only for her. You'd think this might have tipped her off, if she were guilty of anything. Cambon says the woman seemed not to suspect a thing. She took it as flattery that Cambon thought Vincent was the weaker of the couple, not yet composed enough to be subjected to further dredging up of their tragedy. He met her at a restaurant, which seems to be his MO. Do you think the French state pays for his breakfasts, his lunches, his dinners with murder suspects?

— I'm sure of it. Trust me on that.

— The first thing he said to Annette's mother – Cambon looked hard at me when he said this – was that he was convinced the Englishman had killed her daughter. That would be *moi*. He thought this would be a reasonable way of getting her to let down whatever guard she had. It would be the reason for his trip up to Paris, to tell her that he had his man and only needed proof. Now, keep in mind, I was very well aware that as Cambon told me this story, as he described to me how he softened up a suspect in Paris by saying he had his murderer, he was doing precisely the same thing to me at that very moment. Follow me?

— Yes.

— He was introducing a new, firmer suspect – Vincent – and plying me with warm red wine, only to relax me as he had been relaxing Marie-Laure in Paris. He's a *fucking* good detective, Cambon. He was searching my face for guilt, all the while describing Marie-Laure's unbearable grief and supposedly searching *her* face for guilt. He asked her, in the kindest way, if Annette's death had put a strain on her marriage. This elicited the remark he'd hoped for: "There was always strain." "Oh, really? In what way, may I ask?" I can just see Cambon doing this, while simultaneously beckoning the waiter for Madame's refill. He's a charmer, all right. I wonder if he wore his leather jacket in Paris. Probably not. I should have asked. He almost certainly took a suit out of mothballs. He would have upped his accent. Marie-Laure said that the strain had accumulated over time, because of the unusual fact that she'd married Vincent when Annette was just a babe in arms. Had she known Vincent before Annette was born? No. Annette's biological father was a long-standing boyfriend, close friend of the family, had impregnated Marie-Laure on holiday – without knowing it – and then decided he needed to move to New York. He wanted nothing more to do with Marie-Laure, poor woman. She didn't tell the man she was pregnant. She went out and found Vincent. He'd loved her from afar for years. Annette was born, Marie-Laure and Vincent got married, and almost everyone assumed he was the father of the baby girl. Some people live such interesting lives. What are you serving?

— I thought we'd have a glass of something down by my *excellent* pool.

— Lead the way. Cambon's idea here, of course, is that you're the stepfather, you go along with the programme, your wife's daughter starts to become absolutely gorgeous, your testicles begin to throb, you make an advance, hate yourself, panic, kill her, and so on. As I say, what Cambon needed from the mother was a history. Had Vincent ever misbehaved with Annette? How would she know? How could Cambon ask?

— Very gingerly, I'd imagine.

— Yes. Because there was still the possibility that Marie-Laure *was* aware of improper conduct on Vincent's part, and in some sick way was standing by her man even in the direst circumstances.

— Peanut?

— Thank you. From my own experience, I know that Marie-Laure would have been completely unaware of Cambon's strategy. He'd told her the English wanker had done it, right? He was there to console her. To show her what a concerned, humane detective he is. He was so concerned and humane, in fact, that he wanted to know how she and Vincent were getting along in the wake of such an inconceivable tragedy. And if Vincent had "different feelings" about the situation than she did, on account of he wasn't really Annette's father. When you think about it – or at least when Cambon thinks about it – being a stepfather almost *forces* you to kill your stepdaughter. It just seems inevitable. You're not some stalking paedophile, grabbing a stranger off her tricycle. She's living in your house, you're probably allowed to have God knows how much physical contact, and then you snap and go too far, and to cover it up the child must die. Cambon actually told me he thought it would be almost impossible for a stepfather *not* to kill his stepdaughter. Eventually.

— Ridiculous.

— Really? How long did it take you to have your way with Sam?

— Please, Henry. Just stop that. And I wasn't living with him. I wasn't responsible for him.

— I should say not.

— . . .

— Sorry. Anyway, and probably over taxpayers' oysters,

Cambon somehow got Marie-Laure to say that there had been tension in their household as Annette matured. Trust me, Darius, a girl simply doesn't get more beautiful than Annette. Look at what she did to me, and dead at the time. Cambon got Marie-Laure to admit that there was more "distance" between Vincent and Annette, which Cambon thinks means the opposite, from Vincent's point of view. Vincent was afraid of his urges, Cambon says. Annette blossomed, and Vincent couldn't even *talk* to her, he was so aroused. They went on holiday, the sun got to him, he went after Annette in the steaming streets of St-Vuis, he confessed his love, she was appalled, he tried to kiss her, she rejected him, she said she'd tell her mother, and in an ecstatic, murderous embrace, she died.

— You really like that theory, don't you?

— Cambon was hoping I would, that's for sure. He was trying to make me think I was off the hook. But I do – I *really* do – like the theory. You could say I *need* this theory to be true.

— Is that as far as Cambon got, with the mother? That there had been "distance" as Annette grew up?

— He got more. That's how good he is. By the time their coffee arrived he was deep inside the marriage. Vincent had strayed. He took up with a younger woman – he's only our age, by the way. And Cambon said Marie-Laure is thirty-six. Then Vincent did something very bizarre. Out of nowhere, he confessed. Marie-Laure hadn't suspected him at all, and still Vincent felt he had to come out and say that he'd been having an affair with a woman he'd met through his property business – he was selling her late parents' house somewhere. The affair was over, Vincent said. He promised never to do anything like that again. He said he confessed because the guilt was tearing him apart. He begged for forgiveness, and got it.

— That's sort of sweet, thought about a certain way.

— Cambon didn't think so. His idea is that Vincent might have been displacing his lust for Annette, and when the girlfriend didn't satisfy him – she was in her early twenties, by the way – he confessed to his wife just to show her how irresistible he was to younger women. To threaten to take Annette, in other words.

— Far-fetched. Even if Vincent had only implied that, he'd be out on his ear. This is just Cambon optimistically theorising.

— You'd think so. He spent the rest of their time together trying to steer attention away from the English wanker and towards Vincent, in the subtlest way, but Marie-Laure didn't take the bait. And if she's covering up for him, she didn't crack. Cambon hadn't quite got what he'd come for. He's not done with her, though. And he's not done with me.

— So you stayed at the hotel in St-Vuis?

— I did. I went out on the same stroll, drank extremely heavily on the restaurant terrace – same waiter, who didn't recognise me because I'm *so* pulled together this time. Walked up to Annette's hotel, poked about, waited for memories to surface. Found my way back to my hotel. Slept. Nothing. I reported to Cambon in the morning and asked him if I were free to leave. I said I was very sorry, but I couldn't remember anything new. Which wasn't *entirely* the truth.

— Oh?

— I'm shattered. I need to go to bed.

— Don't you want something to eat?

— Thank you, no. I have no appetite. And tomorrow's a big day.

— How so?

— You're going to tell me what to do with my map and I'm going to let you help me be logical about it, Dar. May I call you "Dar"?

— May I call you "Hen"?

— Certainly not. We're going to drink a lot of coffee and see where we stand. Here's the way I see it. I mean, the map part. We can get to the Mary part later. This is very cosy, here. I could get used to it.

— Feel free.

— The way I see it, we've lost Lobke. Porter has queered our pitch. Am I right?

— I think so. I never liked the idea of Lobke anyway. Too overt a crook. We were bound to be double-crossed one way or the other.

— We don't know if Porter has contacted the cardinal. We don't know if Porter's contacted Manny.

— May I make a suggestion? You said yesterday you wanted my help in this.

— Go ahead.

— Henry, if I were you I'd get on the phone to Manny and see if he'll hold at his price – or at any price, really. Hope Porter hasn't already intervened, do a deal *immediately*. Either that or stop the whole thing, which would be my real advice if I thought you'd take it. Keep your phone on in case Porter calls. Make a deal with him. Cut him in on the map. That must be what he wants, since he seems to know all about it. If Manny's still hot for it, I'll have Sam bring him the map. Sam has keys to my flat. He'll do what I say. He won't ask any questions. You could end this part today.

— Wow, aren't you *manly* all of a sudden.

— There's something more which makes me think you have to pull everything together.

— What's that?

— After you went to bed last night, Mary rang. I didn't know if I wanted to tell you this, if I *should* tell you this. I don't know quite how to . . .

— Give it to me.

— Mary heard from Porter.

— Oh, God. I mean, again?

— Yes, Henry. As you suspected, Porter was the one who told her about you and Sophie last week. And now he's told her about Annette.

— Oh, hell. He didn't, by any chance, also tell her that I'm on the verge of making a fortune with a stolen map?

— Not that she mentioned. I'm sorry, Henry, but it gets worse. Mary's told people. She's told, in fact, everyone she knows, and they've told everyone they know. About the affair, about Annette – even about the French detective who thinks you're a murderer. Everyone knows. It's the talk of her world. She wanted it that way.

— You did stress that I've had a nervous breakdown?

— I tried my best. I think that may only have confirmed to her that you were capable of all these terrible things.

— You didn't tell her I'm here with you?

— No. She could guess that all on her own.

— I see. So you're the one nursing me back to mental health.

— That's the way it is now being presented.

— Let me just . . . Let me just come to *grips* with this for a moment or two. I'll do what you say. I'll call Manny if you just . . . Give me a few minutes. Go on and prepare Sam for the delivery. Can't waste any time. To hell with the Vatican. *Fuck* the Vatican. I don't trust them any more than I trust Lobke. Manny's our boy. And my guess is that Porter *will* have got to Manny. I'm sure it was Porter, or one of his associates, outside Manny's house that day. I'll have to think about this. I think . . . You know what? I think Manny would go for the map anyway. What does he care where it came from? He just *needs* it. That's all.

— You know . . . You're going to have a hard time going home, I have a feeling. For a while.

— I know, I know.

— And I don't just mean home. I mean England.

— I understand. You've been through this, in your smaller way.

— It wasn't that small, Henry. I won't argue about what I did being either wrong or just stupid or – my preference – a completely perfect act of love that neither of us would have wanted to live without. Private society says I pay a price. I've had to accept that. I know that Sam's fine, I know exactly what Sam thinks. But I've been punished – far more severely than I've even hinted to you. And now you get your dose. It's the way the world is. If you want to flout the rules, well, join the club. Stay here with me. We'll flout them together.

— There's a thought.

—We'll be defiant.

— Will we give lots of dinner parties for your friends in the village? I can see it now, me having to jump up from aperitifs and flutteringly say, "Ooo, I can smell my *endives* burning." We'll have to clarify matters with the locals.

— If you say so. Now go on, Henry. Make your call. You'll feel better. We'll be able to relax on one front, at least.

— All right. I'll make the call in the kitchen, all right? Don't eavesdrop. I want to tell you the news in full.

— Go on, I say.

— . . .

— Right. Here we go, Dar. The news is, Manny bought the map.

— That's fantastic. This is great news. Are we rich *again*? Ah, but I can tell from your expression that the price went down. Did it?

— Yes.

— How far down?'

— Manny has agreed to purchase the Pilgrim Map for one hundred and fifty-five thousand pounds. Right away. In cash.

— Well, come on, Henry. This is thrilling. It's not your one and a half, it's a tenth of what you'd hoped for, but, for God's sake, after all this, that's a fortune. And the deal is done? Cheer up, man.

— I'm glad it's going to Manny, that's where the map belongs. I like Manny.

— Then why so gloomy? Come *on*, Henry, let's celebrate.

— You can go ahead and get Sam to pick up the map at your flat and deliver it to Manny's house.

— And how will we get the money?

— A bit of a rub, there.

— Why?

— Because Manny has bought the map from Ralph Stenniman.

— What?

— Porter got to him. The deal is that Manny gets the map, Stenniman gets one hundred and fifty-thousand pounds, and we get . . . immunity. No one's the wiser.

— Oh. That's a terrible let-down. I'm so sorry.

— I think Manny must like me, too. He's not going to tell Stenniman where he found the map – not that Stenniman won't guess, but there won't be proof. Manny's going to spare me, let me go straight. I mean, otherwise I'd never work again. So he must like me.

— Good old Manny.

— Go on and ring Sam, if you would. Let's get this over with. He's to deliver the map to Manny's wife, at Manny's house, any time this afternoon. If that's possible.

— . . .

— Did you reach Sam?

— Yes. And he's in London. He'll drop off the map at about three o'clock.

— Good boy.

— He sends his regards.

— You told him I'm here?

— No reason not to. Whom would he tell, and why? He remembers you from last year.

— Did you ever tell him that I . . . ?

— No, no. Of course not. He was horrified enough when his mother found us, as you can imagine. Poor Sam. He's come out of it well, though. Now listen. I want you – I want both of us – to look on the bright side of this development.

— Which is?

— That we're not going to be arrested, of course. And, as you say, you can stay in the business. I just don't think we were cut out for a life of crime. No good at it.

— Speak for yourself. I thought I was *rolling* along. I think I may cry.

— Don't cry, Henry. I'll take you out for an enormous lunch.

— We don't have enough money.

— Let me worry about that. I can keep us going for quite a long time, in fact. Credit is a marvellous thing, when you're a property baron.

— Long enough for Mary to come to her senses?

— Maybe not that long.

— You know, don't you, that pretty soon I'm going to start telling you how much I miss my girls, how guilty I feel about having fucked up Mary's life, how useless I am.

— I know. And I'll start pouring wine into you. Let's make an effort to talk about other things. About our future.

— Good idea, but impossible. You're going to have to endure some emotion from my end. Perhaps I'll have that nervous breakdown, after all. I mean, *fuck* Porter. He's probably taking a cut of the map from Stenniman.

— I know it isn't easy, but you have to put it out of your mind. It's over. It isn't your problem anymore. You've got away with what could have been an awful blunder. You'll have time to pick up the pieces. Forget lunch, then. Let's go for a nice long drive, and bring a bottle. Come now, Esmeralda awaits.

— . . .

— Henry, are you all right? Christ.

— I think so. Jesus.

— Let me help you up. Bloody gravel. Sure you're OK?

— I think I . . . Just scraped my hip. And my elbow. How's the bike?

— Unwell in the first place. Good thing she can't go very fast. I'm sorry about that. Stupid. Drunk, probably. Never happened before. No one saw us, I don't think. How embarrassing if I'd crashed in the village. Never hear the end of it. Let's get us inside for first aid. Esmeralda won't start. We'll leave her here. Come into the kitchen. We'll bandage each other.

— Where are you hurt?

— Same as you.

— We'll live.

— Here we are. I keep this kit for when guests' kiddies cut or scrape themselves. I've had no visitors since the time you were here, of course.

— None?

— No one from the old circle. A pariah is what I am. That's what I'll call my memoirs: *Pariah*. How much wine shall we drink?

— Three bottles.

— Oh, yes, look at the time. It's cocktail hour.

— At least we don't have to eat anymore. Some brandy, too, by the fire, then straight to bed, would be my suggestion.

— There, Henry, you're all patched up. Now do me.

— I wish we had our motorbike crash on film. A couple of gay, drunk Englishmen in their French chateau drive, taken down by a deep patch of gravel. One of your labourers will see the bike, the whole village will know. I've got off on the wrong foot down here.

— Don't worry. It will be your cover story. You've simply moved in with me. I know you can play the part. I'll teach you.

— Am I the boy or the girl? I mean, isn't that how it works? I'd always thought that's how it worked.

— Sometimes. No one's going to *ask*, but for the sake of argument let's say you can be as masculine as you want. And I'll be me.

— You're not effeminate.

— Yes, I am, just not in front of you. I have to clench my jaw all the time, talking to you. Even now – especially because I must be quite drunk – it's a physical effort not to shriek with girlish laughter at what just happened to us.

— Don't you have a boyfriend you're not telling me about? Someone to replace Antoine?

— Er . . . Well. For a while I rekindled an old flame – you've never met him. Here, be the man and light a fire. I'll fetch the bottle and glasses. Yes, my old flame. He was a writer once. He had a success with *Gregory,* about fifteen years ago. You wouldn't have heard of it. No one has. It was based on me, if you want to know the truth. When we became reacquainted – right here, in fact – I found him depressed and depressing. All his spirit had drained away. And he was overweight. I can't bear that. When he told me he lived with his parents, and when he asked me for money, well . . .

— Is the idea to wait for Sam to grow up?

— That is definitely *not* the idea.

— We're turning forty next year, the two of us. Perhaps we should throw a joint party here?

— Oh, *good* idea. Shall we start making a guest list? Your man Rory might show. Father Anthony could pop over from Rome. You'll find the social life's something of a desert, after the fall.

— I have to lie low, that's what you're saying. I get your point – that I'm lucky with the Stenniman deal. Stupid, stupid, stupid. Why did you encourage me?

— It wasn't like that. It was the opposite. I agreed to help because I'm your friend.

— You're my *best* friend.

— Thank you.

— You're my *only* friend.

— Well, then, there we are. Let's drink to good old Manny.

— And to Martha.

— You ought to be pleased, Henry. On that score, at least. You were being toyed with by these people, except for Manny. They would have ruined your career, or worse.

— Some career. And to think that goofy, ignorant Andreas is back in the business.

— You could be partners again.

— Never. We were always incompatible. He was too impetuous, I was too cautious. We should have complemented each other, but it was a bad mix. To go for one big hit like the Hawaii was suicidal. Hubris, is what it was. I should have learned from Rory Fine, long ago, that you have to build, build, build. You need a foundation.

— Well, then, that's what you'll do now. Of course you'll be slowed down by the vampires at Child Support.

— Don't talk that way. Mary will come round. She'll see the glamour in what I've been doing. In fact it occurred to me during lunch that if I tell her about the Pilgrim Map adventure, she'll fall in love with me all over again. They love a scoundrel, women. Don't they?

— I'm not the one to ask. I've read that it's so. I've also read that they like what's known as "support", which would include things like money, fidelity, emotional tenderness and physical love. It's a hell of a job, sounds like to me. Look how quickly we finished that bottle . . .

— What do your sort need? Tell me the truth.

— That would take some thought. Considering that just over a year ago I was telling you I'd found "the one", and I was sincerely prepared to stay the course, and I was most definitely in love, and Antoine walked away as if he'd never known me, well . . .

— And that you were having your way with Sam on the same day you told me you'd found "the one" with Antoine – I get the picture.

— I don't want you to think I'm sad. Or that I drink so much with you to make the pain go away. I feel relatively calm about life. The usual way of handling the sort of difficulty I've faced is to say that the people who abandoned me weren't real friends. That would be, let's see – everybody.

— You have me.

— I have you. And I'm grateful for that. Who do you think will stand by you? Your brother?

— He's long gone from my world, and has been for many years. You're probably thinking I went through all of this as a way of getting back at Colin, or catching him up. If he could be a hero, I could be a rogue. And you'd be right, to an extent. But I insist it was mainly Mary. How much pressure was I supposed to take? Why couldn't I be like Peter, like Justin, like Bernard, like Robert? All *her* friends, mind you. Why couldn't I leave the house in the morning and return in the evening with so much money she didn't know where to begin wasting it? Is that a way to live? Well, it is for Mary's crowd.

— To be fair, Henry, you would have if you could have. What if things had been different, the Hawaii had turned out to be what you thought it was, one deal led to another, and you were another Rory Fine right now? It just didn't happen. If there wasn't failure, how would people judge success?

— That's supposed to make me feel better?

— The only option is to reject their standards. I thought that was what our friendship was all about, twenty years ago. You've said it yourself, Henry, that if you fall you have to adapt to where you've fallen. It's your failed-banker-turned-Buddhist argument.

— I'm no Buddhist. I'm a nothing, at this moment. Pour me some more of that. Is this what we're going to do, just drink by the fire?

— There'll be a lot of that.

— Suits me, I suppose.

— You'll get back into maps. You'll work hard. I'll work hard. I know that deep down you like the map trade. Sam will have delivered the Pilgrim Map to Manny by now, thanks to you.

— Yes, thanks to me. And thanks to my . . . impromptu theft. I can see Manny now. Martha will have brought the map into the study. Manny will have taken it out of the velvet sleeve, just glanced at it with his camera eyes, put it back in the sleeve, wandered down to the empty slot in his bookcase, slid the object in there, and gone back to his berry wine and his antique chess games. He'll probably never look at it again. He just has to know it's there. You don't have to show off, if you're that wealthy, not like George Burling, or Lobke. I suppose that's what I like about Manny. He found his thing, and lived it to the hilt. The thought of his contentment makes me feel *slightly* better.

— I hate to ask, but has occurred to you to ring Sophie? She *may* be wondering what's going on.

— I'm far too pissed to do that now. And yes, it has occurred to me. I'd just say . . . Well, I guess I'd ask her to understand. It's not as if I can't be replaced, for a woman like her. I'll never in a million years figure out why she . . .

— What.

— Never mind.

— Come on, Henry.

— Well, obviously, why she approached me in the first place.

— You might have been sending off some signals. You can't honestly tell me it was the first time.

— I told you it was.

— I know you did. And I didn't believe you.

— Why didn't you believe me?

— People talk, Henry.

— What?

— Listen, I don't even circulate directly with Mary's crowd, and I'd heard of at least two indiscretions that were common knowledge.

— Oh, for Christ's—

— Angela someone, was it? And an Asian-sounding name of a married woman? Ring a bell?

— Who told you this?

— Third, even fourth-hand people. Look, just think of the dirt you've got on practically everyone you know. And step back for a moment and realise they've all got the same on you. There's practically nothing you've done and wanted to keep secret that isn't the currency of gossip behind your back. You must have known that, at least intellectually. It only makes sense.

— In a horrible way it does. Thanks for pointing that out, Dar.

— So will you ring Sophie?

— Maybe it would be a better idea if you did that for me. Introduce yourself as a close friend of Mr Hart, tell her the same story we're telling Mary. I've had an emotional crack-up, I'm out of the country, you're looking after me. She shouldn't expect to hear from me for a long time. Would you do that?

— I could do that, yes. In fact, I'll do it right now. I'm that can-do sort of person, as you've seen. You stay here with your bottle and I'll be right back.

— . . .

— I didn't speak to her for long. She was on her way out the door. I told her the necessary.

— How did she sound?

— Perky. In a rush. Not . . . *especially* worried about you. She said to thank you for the pin. I don't think she expects to hear from you again, ever.

— She said that?

— Not in so many words. It's possible, of course, that this sort of thing has happened to her before. Maybe not with the nervous-breakdown excuse—

— It's not an excuse. This *is* a nervous breakdown. And I'm a drunk, look at me. The room is starting to spin. I hate this. I hope I'm not going to be sick. Just one more, and I should go to bed. *Look* at those bottles. Tomorrow I will abstain. Thank you, by the way, for making the call. What would I do without you? And don't let me go *near* the telephone. I'd just call Mary and ask to speak to the girls and cry and make a fool of myself. Again. You don't have any cigars, do you?

— Sorry, no. And you don't smoke cigars.

— Blech. Gah. What *am* I doing? I don't think brandy's the

thing to stave off the old *Weltschmerz*, do you? I really think I need to go to bed. Mary's probably got the girls to sleep by now. She'll be in our stinking little kitchen with a girlfriend, sipping too-expensive wine, *frying me in oil*. Every goddamned thing I've ever done will be d— . . . Excuse me. Dredged up. How can I win? How was I ever going to win? Is she perfect? Is her *approach* a valid one? A king's ransom for a bloody education? Schools, schools, schools. Fuck 'em. Clothes, cars, ski trips, fuck 'em.

— That's the spirit, Henry.

— Property ladder, my arse.

— Too right.

— Nightmare.

— Speaking of which, how's the old foot-liver dream going?

— All clear. Worse ones now. A reason it's important to be pissed before bed. Let me just— Woah.

— Henry?

— Did I just fall out of my chair?

— Let me help you.

— Oh, this is terrific. Legless in France.

— Let's get you to bed. I don't want you trying the stairs on your own.

— Too kind, too kind. Here we go. Woopsie. Thanks. I'll just bring the bottle. Here we go. Really.

— I'll get the door. There we are. Let's get you out of your clothes.

— Those dreams, was that what I was talking about? No foot-liver now. But Annette? She's still there, all right, oh yes she is. Undead and a little older. A lot of Annettes.

— There were others? Lie down, now.

— Others? Aw. In my youth. You know, all those girlfriends I had in the old days, when I was on the road, how much fun I was having?

— Yes.

— Not true. Not true. Never happened. I'd be – I don't know –

I'd be in Germany, spend a long day with the maps, empty or fill up the car boot, and off I'd go to get a girl.

— You paid?

— Yes, I— What are you doing?

— I'm not leaving you alone, Henry. Lie back and relax.

— Yes, I paid. After the first time, everything made sense, and I got very comfortable with the idea. I have never, in my whole life, until just now, told *anyone* this. Not that I'm ashamed. But if you're a punter, you know, for a long time, best to do it out of sight. Some people think it's wrong, which it *isn't*. Just *isn't*. You've had your share, I bet, you and a couple of rent boys, right? That's what you lot do.

— No.

— Come on, I've confessed.

— I'm not crazy.

— Oh, gotcha. Disease. What are you doing?

— Just making you comfortable. Relax.

— So I like young blonde girls. Always did, since I was a child, still do, always will. Frozen. They're just frozen, right in here. There's nothing *I* can do about it. Who cares? What's wrong with that? It just *is*. So what if I'm a degenerate? What does it mean? So I'm a degenerate . . . I never raped anyone. I never . . . There was a rule of thumb. The kind of girl I wanted cost exactly the same amount of money as a solid meal and a bottle of wine. So I went hungry, in one way. I was completely in control. And you've got to understand, these weren't streetwalkers, these weren't the girls in windows. These were students, for the most part. Expensive. Very much the sort of girl I would have been dating at twenty, if I'd known how to do that. I learned to be demanding. I knew whom to ask. I wanted clean hair. I wanted to peel open a girl's silk kimono. That sort of thing. Never the same girl more than two or three times. How many? I don't know the answer. And I loved, I *loved* it every single time.

— Why on earth did you get married?

— Just trying to be nice. And I'm no monster. I've told you what I like. Maybe you like posh sixteen-year-old boys – I mean, you've made that awfully damned clear to the whole world. Do you think the little detective is right, and Vincent freaked out and killed Annette?

— Yes.

— I bloody well hope so. You know, I just had a feeling . . . Cambon wasn't crazy to make me retrace my steps, to catch me out having followed her, to have me spend a night in the terrible hotel room.

— Did you remember something?

— It's more that I didn't remember . . . remembering. I must have been pickled head to toe. I mean, I did follow her and her parents. And maybe I did hang around, just longingly, regretfully. Wondering what to do. Maybe wondering if I could find an itsy-bitsy red-light district in that town. Relive the golden years. It wasn't that late at night. So the thought certainly must have occurred to me.

— But you don't remember?

— I . . . don't.

— Do you remember seeing Annette coming out of the hotel alone?

— I . . . do. But it's more that the memory has been implanted. I've thought about it so much, it's as if it happened. It's the guilt, Dar, the guilt. And your fault for making me so overheated I thought I could drink down the urge, you know? Stop that, would you?

— You have to relax, so you can sleep. You don't want me to stop.

— Stop.

— OK, all right.

— When I took up Cambon on his experiment, and walked to my hotel from where Annette and her parents were staying, I didn't recognise a thing. I got lost, in fact. I must have had a blackout the last time, is what I'm saying. Is that possible? Is it alcoholic amnesia? Could I have wandered all the way back to that room, let myself in, and not remembered a thing the next morning? I mean, it's a ten-minute walk at most.

— You had some sort of heatstroke. While pissed. I'm sure that's what happened. You had no reason, at the time, to *try* to remember. You were oblivious.

— Theoretically, I could have killed Annette. Theoretically.

— Don't think that way then. Of course you didn't kill anyone.

— How do I know?

— Because Cambon thinks he's got his man. And anyway if you were so out of it that night, how would you have disposed of her clothes? Put it away, Henry; it wasn't you. It was a coincidence. You're only feeling guilty because of the impulse.

— I wish you'd stop.

— No, you don't. Relax. Close your eyes.

— Don't make me beg.

— Relax. You'll be asleep soon.

— You will fucking *stop* that. *Now*. Don't make me hit you.

— Let me just show you— *Ow!*

— I said I'd hit you.

— God, I've wanted this for so long. I've wanted you for so long.

— Keep away from me, Saddler. Sit over there. Jesus.

— All right. Be calm. I'm going.

— No, you sit down. Something occurred to me. You've rather wiped it from my mind. Pass the bottle, it's on the floor.

— Here you are.

— Thank you.

— You'll think of whatever it is in the morning.

— In the morning, after this? What the hell did you think you were trying to do?

— Don't be silly. You're fine.

— No, it's right there. Oh. Yes, I think I have it. Nagging away at me. You have to explain a couple of things to me. And I have to think about what you say.

— Lie still.

— Oh my . . . Hey. Oh my *God.*

— What now?

— Oh, man. Must . . . Saddler, you . . .

— What is it?

— How did you . . . How did you know where to send Sam? How did you know Manny's address?

— You told me. You told me St Alban's Grove.

— No, but . . . The number. The house. You knew it.

— You described the house. What are you saying? Try to relax. You're going to have to sleep. Get comfortable.

— Don't come near me. Stay where you are.

— You need to sleep, Henry.

— You . . . Wait a fucking . . . You knew Sophie's telephone number, just now. You did. You *did.*

— . . .

— You're fucking . . .

— Relax. Just calm yourself, Henry. Don't try to sit up. You've had a hell of a lot to drink. You've got to close your eyes.

— You're . . .

— Please don't say it. You'll ruin everything. Don't say it.

— You're Porter.

— . . .

— You're *Porter.*

— And you're hallucinating.

— Like hell.

— Relax. You're with me, now. You're with Saddler.

— You crazy *bastard.*

— All right.

— You set up Sophie?

— That's . . . a way to put it.

— You did that? You made that happen?

— I asked her to give you her card. That's all.

— And to say, "I want to know you better"?

— That was her line. I didn't even know her. I swear, I've never met her. I just wanted to give you the option. I mean, *you* were the one who called her up a few weeks later. You went in with your eyes wide open.

— But you . . . You *paid* her? You paid her, didn't you?

— Put it this way: she won a bet of sorts. She was betting you'd call her up and start an affair. So I paid her, yes. I didn't know beforehand that I'd *have* to. It was all well-intentioned, believe me. I've always been on your side.

— You wanted to ruin my marriage, obviously.

— What marriage? I've been pointing this out. You've admitted as much, without saying so. You never loved Mary. You loved me.

— Don't be ridiculous. What, this has been festering away for years?

— For twenty-nine years, to be exact.

— But *nobody* likes me. What do *you* like about me, then?

— I like your enthusiasm. I think you can let go.

— This is impossible. I'm just trying to think. To what extent . . . To what *extent* are you Porter?

— There's only the one.

— The accents, the drops, the following around?

— All.

— You're . . . *grotesque*.

— Sleep on it, Henry. It will all make sense. I think it already does. I was simply your conscience. Think of it that way.

— How did you know about St-Vuis?

— I told you. I saw it in the paper. You told me you were going there. And you never rang. I thought—

— What, you *immediately* jumped to the conclusion that your old friend murdered a little girl? Is that what it was about?

— No, no. I thought it was strange that something like that had happened, and you didn't ring me. This is weeks later, Henry. Just silence from your end – I didn't know at the time that you'd been freaked out by the Sam episode. You didn't even ring to thank me for inviting you. Nothing. So I just wondered. And I made a phone call.

— To whom?

— To the police. Anonymously. I said I might have something to contribute to the investigation.

— You . . . Get *out*.

— Listen. I was curious.

— Get *out* of here.

— I didn't mention your name, or anything. I was told that unless I had something concrete to offer, the investigation was secret. So I just said, "The Englishman," and whoever it was on the line said, "Yes? What about him?" And I rang off.

— And you started blackmailing me.

— It wasn't like that. I just tested the waters. I was curious.

— You could have *asked* me.

— It got out of control. And it was . . . You were right from the start, Henry. It was Mary as well. Once this all got started, it was the two of us, seeing how far you'd go.

— You took my *money*.

— I have your money. It's yours. Unspent.

— Terrific.

— May I get in bed? I'll just lie right here while you sleep. I won't touch you, promise.

— I'm not going to *sleep* with you. I mean, for fuck's *sake*.

— I know you're angry, but—

— *Angry?*

— Look, *you* had an affair, *you* stole the map, *you* flounced around flogging it to the bloody Vatican, *you* dyed your hair, *you* paid blackmail, *you* . . .

— The map was never any good.

— What?

— The map's a piece of shit. Just thought I'd tell you that.

— What?

— The map's just a *nothing*. I knew that from the start. I'm the *punter*, remember? I'm the *wanker*. But I'm smart enough to know one thing: Paris, 1928, just as I told you it might be. Super-fine electric diamond drill. Anyone who cared could have figured that out. I did. Anyone who paid more than ten grand for that . . . that . . . *curiosity*, would be mad.

— Mad Manny.

— Precisely.

— When were you going to tell me that?

— When were you going to tell me you were Porter?

— Never, if I could get away with it. Oh, and it really is quite a lot of money I owe you from the extortion. You'll have it first thing in the morning, in the original envelopes. I was going to pay that back, one way or the other, I promise. Are you all right?

— It's just hitting me. You . . .

— Go ahead and cry. You've been through a lot.

— If you don't get your fucking hands off me . . . Get out. Get out, Saddler. Leave me alone.

— I won't—

— *Out*. And leave the bottle where it is.

## The following morning, eight o'clock

Darius Saddler, wearing lavender pyjamas, noiselessly walks down the corridor to the guest bedroom where Henry Hart has slept. He knocks gently but gets no reply. He tries the door, but it is locked from the inside.

—Hart? Henry? I'm coming in. Are you there? Why's the door locked . . .? Look, Henry, we'll talk this through. Sorry I . . . rushed things. We were drunk. And I'm sorry I . . . deceived you. I truly am. Can I come in? I didn't want to wake you, but Cambon was on the phone. Detective Cambon. He wouldn't tell me everything. Can you hear me? Come on, don't make me break the door down. Don't sulk. It sounds like good news. I'm sure he's got his man. Henry? He said you'd be *très content*. Henry? I said don't make me break the door down. I just had it painted. Why have you locked the door? Henry? Can you hear me? I can explain a lot of things. I think I can explain *everything*. Henry? Oh, my God. Oh, no. No, Henry! I'm breaking down the door, now. Henry? Jesus. Henry? Where are you? Oh, God. Henry, are you in the bathroom? Speak to me. I'll break *this* door down. I'll call the police. I'm calling an ambulance *now*. Are you in there? Oh, my God. Oh, my God. Shit.

— Saddler?

— Henry!

— Can't a chap vomit in peace in this chateau?

— Jesus. Open the fucking door.

— Will you give me just the tiniest moment to wash my face? Brew us some coffee and I'll be right down.

— . . .

— Well, good *morning,* darling.

— Henry, for Christ's sake.

— Have you stepped out for croissants yet?

— You scared the life out of me.

— Oh? How did *that* feel, you miserable *fuck*?

— Jesus, I thought you'd—

— I had the feeling you might. I've always wanted to fake my own death, even for a minute. How *did* that feel? Sorry about the doors, but it was worth it.

— I really thought you'd—

— Well, *good.* And I suppose that would have suited you, yes? As an outcome? You completely *fuck* with my life, you trick me down here, you . . . you try to have your pathetic *way* with me after pouring booze down my throat all day, and then, you know, if I'd done the deed, cut my wrists, hanged myself from the door knob, whatever you thought I'd done, that would be *perfect,* wouldn't it? Maybe you'd do a Juliet and kill yourself right along with me? A perfect love story. Is that what you wanted?

— Nothing of the kind, I—

— Do you think I even *slept,* last night? After that . . . It really is wonderful to know that you're even crazier than I am. You are utterly *sick.* You give queers everywhere a bad name. Are you *all* so insane? And don't say it. Don't *say* it. I can see your queer lips forming the words. "But I . . . *love* you." You maniac. You *are* a maniac. Delicious coffee, by the way. *Gay* coffee. So there I was last night, for hours, piecing your crimes together. Lying there, wanting to murder you, nauseated. Thank *God* you didn't . . . I mean I would have torn your cock out by its *roots*. Thinking about you twirling on your heel in the dark outside Manny's house. That *was* you?

— Yes.

— Slinking around in my street?

— No. You were imagining that.

— Good to see you looking so contrite, you queer *fuck*.

— Such language.

— I looked in on you last night. Passed out sideways on the bed. And *smiling*. I took a shower and sobered up and thought about what I'd do.

— You're going to kill me. Are you going to kill me? Please don't kill me.

— I wouldn't know how. I only strangle little girls, right?

— I never thought you did, I promise. I just . . . I got out of control. *You* got out of control. The map – you don't *steal*, Henry, that's just wrong. Stenniman deserved his money, Manny deserved his map. Everybody's happy. I . . . *facilitated* this.

— Everybody's happy? *Look* at me.

— You were always going to leave Mary.

— Yes, but not for *you*, you *moron*.

— I thought I'd made my intentions clear. I mean, for decades now. Hadn't I? Why all the games, Henry?

— You keep *saying* that. Games? Why do you keep *saying* that?

— Have you decided anything, then, if you're not going to kill me?

— You'll be punished, that's for sure. I haven't thought that through. As for the family – well, I'll simply join the ranks of the divorced, like everyone else. There isn't a huge problem there, really. I'll get over that particular guilt in no time. In ten years my daughters will throw themselves at me, they'll hate Mary for remarrying, they'll hate the stepfather, naturally. He'll be *awful*. This is guaranteed. The girls will love their rogue papa. So on that front everything takes care of itself. It's something to look forward to. As for you, you bastard, I'm going to make you *pay*. I haven't had a chance to write down a list of the things I'm going to have you do, but it starts with you keeping your filthy, depraved, gay-queer-homo-pederast hands the fuck *off* of me, unless for some unforeseen reason I *specifically* request otherwise.

— Done.

— I'll be needing a beautiful girlfriend, which you will arrange. You will be my pimp. Is that achievable at all? I mean with all my blackmail money stored up, you should be able to sort out something along the lines of a beautiful girlfriend for me, as early as today. Be my pimp.

— I know where to ask.

— Fine. And your house over the bridge. I will be living there.

— You don't want to—

— I will be living there, with my youthful blonde companions, until you sell the place.

— Agreed.

— Well, aren't you easy. You'd do anything for me, wouldn't you?

— Yes.

— I'm going to need your car. I'm going to be driving around trading maps. Because I'm *good* at it.

— Take my car.

— You'll be fronting me ten grand to get me started.

— I can raise that.

— Mary will be remarried in about a year and a half, I'm guessing, to someone wealthy enough to let me off the hook financially. I will throw myself into my work, and I will be a millionaire in ten years – about the time my girls come rushing back into my arms. Rogue Papa. If you haven't sold this chateau yet, I'll take it off your hands at an *extortionate* discount.

— I can't wait.

— I'll think of further penance as time goes on. This is a start, at least. It occurred to me last night that the most generous way of looking at what you've done is you've restored the pact. Is that where we are? Have we dropped out now, at last? Are we outlaws?

— Seems so.

— To the extent that I will ever trust myself with a decision again, I'm happy with this one. I'm not going to *thank* you, Saddler, so don't get your hopes up. You can do your self-justification routine later on. I can hear it already. You precipitated what was going to happen to me anyway. You saved me from prison. You arranged a welcome sexual affair. You acted out of affection – no, out of *love*. Eventually I'll tell you I love you, too. Aw, look, you're blushing. You are so *abject*, Saddler. We'll sit by the fire like a couple of old queens, and we'll smile at the memory of our blind adventure. Good. Rogue Papa set up with a queer in the South of France. I'll be like Lobke. I can live with this idea, Saddler. Sure. It's a reasonable outcome. It's what you want, it's what I want. You find yourself where you fall, right? We'll make the best of it. That's what I say. I'm perfectly content. I haven't changed. You *obviously* haven't changed. The way I see things now, that other world can go to the devil without me.